## "Incoming!"

Gabe grabbed the shotgun that had been resting in the overhead rack.

Tara's gun, which had been tucked into Gabe's waistband for safekeeping, slid away from his back as the US deputy marshal retrieved it.

"How sure are you they're after us?" she called out as her niece awoke with a startled cry.

The tractor's rearview mirror showed the massive vehicle chewing up the yards. Seconds before the Hummer would have rammed their back end, the vehicle swept wide around them, then roared ahead. Hope spurted that they had not been the target after all.

The Hummer whipped a sliding turn that whirled the vehicle 360 degrees and then some, finally coming to rest side-on, blocking traffic. Blocking *them*. Four hulking menaces brandishing automatic weapons sprang through open doors and set up firing stances in their direction.

Gabe brought the tractor to a halt in the middle of the road. The *put-put-put* of the diesel engine marked time, like an eerie metronome, in the sudden, ominous inertia.

"Oh, I'm very certain they're after us. One hundred percent."

**Jill Elizabeth Nelson** writes what she likes to read—faith-based tales of adventure seasoned with romance. Parts of the year find her and her husband on the international mission field. Other parts find them at home in rural Minnesota, surrounded by the woods and prairie and their four grown children and young grandchildren. More about Jill and her books can be found at jillelizabethnelson.com or Facebook.com/jillelizabethnelson.author.

**Books by Jill Elizabeth Nelson**

**Love Inspired Suspense**

*Evidence of Murder*
*Witness to Murder*
*Calculated Revenge*
*Legacy of Lies*
*Betrayal on the Border*
*Frame-Up*
*Shake Down*
*Rocky Mountain Sabotage*
*Duty to Defend*
*Lone Survivor*
*The Baby's Defender*
*Hunted for Christmas*
*In Need of Protection*
*Unsolved Abduction*
*Hunted in Alaska*
*Safeguarding the Baby*
*Targeted for Elimination*
*Texas Revenge Target*
*Wyoming Wilderness Survival*
*Danger in the Desert*
*Peril in the Rockies*

Visit the Author Profile page at LoveInspired.com.

# PERIL IN THE ROCKIES

JILL ELIZABETH NELSON

LOVE INSPIRED SUSPENSE
INSPIRATIONAL ROMANCE

MIX
Paper | Supporting responsible forestry
FSC® C021394
FSC www.fsc.org

LOVE INSPIRED® SUSPENSE
INSPIRATIONAL ROMANCE

Recycling programs for this product may not exist in your area.

ISBN-13: 978-1-335-91923-6

Peril in the Rockies



For questions and comments about the quality of this book, please contact us at CustomerService@Harlequin.com.



Love Inspired
22 Adelaide St. West, 41st Floor
Toronto, Ontario M5H 4E3, Canada
www.LoveInspired.com

HarperCollins Publishers
Macken House, 39/40 Mayor Street Upper,
Dublin 1, D01 C9W8, Ireland
www.HarperCollins.com

**Printed in Lithuania**

1 2 3 4 5 6 7 8 9 10 LIT 29 28 27 26

Therefore shall ye lay up these my words in your heart and in your soul, and bind them for a sign upon your hand, that they may be as frontlets between your eyes. And ye shall teach them your children, speaking of them when thou sittest in thine house, and when thou walkest by the way, when thou liest down, and when thou risest up.

—*Deuteronomy* 11:18–19

To the many responsible and loving parents who do their best to bring their children up to respect God, live with integrity and love people

# ONE

A shrill screech rang through the kitchen, setting Tara Markson's hair on end. The splat of food hitting the floor quickly followed, along with a wail of astonishing volume from the petite toddler perched in the high chair. Tara blinked against the sting of tears. She was failing as a mother.

Little wonder. Tara *wasn't* this child's mother. She was a mere stand-in for her sister, the child's real mother. But Tara was all her niece had now that Linnea was gone and not coming back. A burn crept up Tara's esophagus. Thanks to her sister's murdering scum of an ex-husband, Linnea would never get to see her daughter grow up. That privilege now fell to Tara—if she could get little Sofie to eat and not starve to death.

Tara unfurled the fingers that had formed unconsciously into fists. "It's okay, Sofie." She forced soothing notes into her tone. "I know you miss her, and you don't have the words to talk about it."

She unsnapped the food-smeared toddler from the high chair and hugged her quivering body close. Sofie buried her messy face in Tara's shoulder and continued sobbing.

Tara rubbed circles on the child's back. "You've got to

be massively confused about where your mama has gone. Me, too, kid. Me, too."

Not that she was confused about *why* Linnea wasn't here. She understood death's finality in a way that this child couldn't. Not yet. But she *was* confused about how Linnea ever got mixed up with Zander in the first place. Sure, the man had been handsome, and he'd oozed charm. But the first time Linnea proudly introduced Zander as her new husband, following a whirlwind romance, Tara's cop senses had clued in on the smarmy vibe beneath the suave exterior.

Tara hadn't even been invited to the wedding, for pity's sake. Excluding the only family her sister had from such a momentous occasion should have been a significant clue to Linnea right there, but no, she'd allowed herself to be swept off to Vegas—Vegas!—for a quick, slick marriage ceremony. What the perpetually insecure and perennially naive Linnea had considered romantic, Tara had recognized as manipulative and controlling. Linnea had been three years older than Tara, but ever since thirteen years ago—when Lin was twenty and Tara was seventeen—and their parents were killed in the tragic crash of their small plane, Lin had seemed cut adrift and desperately seeking love and acceptance.

For years, Tara had been anchoring her sister through emotional messes and one bad relationship after another, often being resented for what Linnea considered interference, which later turned to grudging gratitude when Tara was there to walk her sister through yet another heartbreak. This time, Lin had plunged into a serious commitment without consulting anybody, leaving Tara feeling unable to voice her opinion, but only to behave as supportively as possible. Her sister was married and pregnant before Tara knew anything about it.

Dread had taken hold inside Tara regarding her sister and this man from that moment on. And now, Tara's worst imaginings had come to pass. Linnea woke up too late to her husband's true nature. Hard to keep the rose-colored glasses on when the man skipped the country because he'd become the focus of a national manhunt for an appalling variety of RICO violations, including violent crimes.

Sure, Linnea had immediately divorced the guy, but she already had an infant that her ruthless ex intended to claim by any means necessary. As proven by the law enforcement investigation after the fact, arranging a hit on his ex-wife for the purpose of kidnapping their baby hadn't stretched Zander's resources at all, even though he was on another continent. Only the hit part had gone to plan, however. Tara, herself, had foiled the baby snatch using her skills as a deputy United States marshal. She was furious with God for allowing her to arrive at her sister's house for a visit moments too late to save Linnea's life, even as she was grateful that Sofie had been spared an existence under the thumb of her criminal father. But unpacking the turmoil of emotions was for later—maybe much later. Tara had a child to raise.

She ran her hand over the soft chestnut curls on her niece's head—a near match for Tara's own thick wavy locks. With a shuddering sniffle, Sofie gazed up at her with the wide brown eyes that ran in the family, including the child's mother and aunt. Tara tickled the girl under the chin, and a wobbly smile formed on the plump little face.

"I think Teddy might be hungry. Shall we feed him?"

The smile split into a white-toothed grin, still lacking a few primary teeth that had yet to come in. Sofie's head bobbed up and down—tears forgotten on her apple cheeks and brown eyes gleaming in anticipation. At sixteen months, Sofie had known numerous individual words, including *yes*, but she'd ceased using them after her mother's disappearance from her life. The child psychologist had advised Tara that time, patience and a stable environment were the best medicines for the linguistic setback.

Tara hated to involve the infamous Teddy in caring for her niece because the stuffed toy had been bought by her reprobate father back before Sofie had even been born and before he'd abandoned his family. But Sofie loved the thing, so Tara would simply have to swallow her revulsion for any object tainted by association with Zander. Sighing, she carried her niece to the living room of her tidy ranch house located about ten minutes outside of Great Falls, Montana, and retrieved the child's beloved teddy bear from the sofa.

Then they went back to the kitchen and sat at the table. Tara held Sofie on her lap while they pretended to feed Teddy, and the toddler contentedly consumed the bites that first went to Teddy's fabric lips and then into her human mouth. The goal was to restore Sofie's ability to feed herself from her own high chair, as she'd been doing for months prior to Linnea's murder, but that day wasn't today. Apparently, Sofie still felt too insecure to eat independently. She needed Tara's lap to feel safe.

Thankfully, as soon as the toddler's tummy was full, her head began to droop, and she let out a loud yawn. Smiling, Tara cleaned her niece's face and hands and then carried her to her crib for her afternoon nap in a small bedroom next to Tara's. For long seconds, she stood beside Sofie's crib and watched the little girl sleep. A yawn mirroring her niece's crept up Tara's throat, but she made it a quiet one. No way was she going to disturb Sofie's rest.

As much as Tara craved joining the little girl in a much-needed nap, she had to take this opportunity to check in with her law enforcement contacts about progress on the prosecution of the hired killer she'd caught standing over her sister's body. In a futile attempt to cast blame elsewhere, the man had confessed to being hired by Zander for what he had done. Tara also needed an update on the manhunt for the fugitive father who'd vanished into Eastern Europe and then into Asia, as well as on the almost nonexistent cooperation from governments in locating Zander Wolf, much less extraditing him if found.

Tara's lip curled at the thought of the criminal's surname. The man was a wolf, all right, and seemed determined to do anything to claim his innocent offspring. Over her dead body would that come true. Tara had done everything she could to prepare for the next attempt to grab Sofie, including installing a sophisticated home security system, but waiting on pins and needles had gotten old fast. Once the guy was behind bars, where he belonged, and cut off from his contacts, then Tara would breathe easily. Not a second before.

Letting out a small disgusted grunt, Tara left the toddler's room. On her way back to the kitchen and her cell phone on the table, the device's ringtone began to play the Otis Redding song, "Respect." That meant her partner, Brennan Greene, from the Marshals Service was calling, probably with the very update she desired. Tara's steps quickened.

She snatched up the phone and put it to her ear. "Hey, Brennan. What do you have for me?"

Puffing breaths answered her. Tara's brows pulled together. Was her partner running?

"You've got to get out of there." *Pant.* "One of my best confidential informants just called." *Pant.* "An armed snatch crew is on the way to your place as we speak." *Pant.* "I'm rolling out momentarily, and I've got sheriff's deputies headed your way. But they won't get there in time." *Pant.* "Grab that baby and run!"

The breath stalled in Tara's lungs as every molecule in her body froze. Noises like someone getting into a vehicle taunted her ears.

"Did you hear me?" Brennan's semi-shout broke Tara's paralysis.

"On it."

Tara pocketed the phone and swung into action, scolding herself for the precious seconds lost while frozen in place. She was trained better than that, but then, she'd never been in a dangerous situation that was so personal in nature. Thankfully, she kept go-bags ready for herself and Sofie at all times. She rushed to her room, grabbed hers and then moved into the nursery and scooped up her niece's.

Moving like a well-oiled automaton, Tara strode through the kitchen and out the mudroom door into the attached garage. Muted scents of motor oil and the paint stored on the shelving teased her nostrils. The late October chill had crept into the compact space, prompting a shiver from her. Ignoring the discomfort, Tara stowed Sofie's bag in the back next to the child safety seat. She climbed behind the wheel, placed her own bag in the passenger seat beside her, and her phone in the cup holder, readily available. A press of the ignition button started her Jeep Grand Cherokee, a hardy four-wheel drive vehicle suited for Montana winters. Then she activated the garage door remote, which obediently began to creep upward.

Not waiting for the action to finish, Tara darted back into the house and donned her winter jacket and stocking cap, but pressed her thick warm gloves into the jacket's pockets. She didn't care to handle the steering wheel while wearing bulky gloves. Nor would they allow her to bundle her niece into her little snowsuit for travel in cold weather.

Tara's gut clenched. Poor Sofie. Her nap was about to be rudely interrupted. Tara could expect lots of loud wailing, but better the child cried in her custody than with a coldhearted crew of kidnappers. The startled bawling happened just as Tara had anticipated, but quickly pressing the infamous Teddy into the child's arms reduced the upset to mild sniffles.

Less than ten minutes after receiving the emergency warning, the Jeep was on the road. Chill gripped the vehicle's atmosphere. The engine hadn't yet warmed up enough to generate heat for the interior. The afternoon sun hung sullenly in a metallic-gray sky.

Tara frowned at the low-slung clouds. The forecast she'd checked this morning had not predicted bad weather. Not that she had any choice about being on the road. At least she had a destination fixed in her mind, one that no one knew about and would be difficult for any pursuer to identify through cyber or even human resources as connected to her. However, reaching the cabin did require her to drive toward the nasty-looking cloud cover and up into the mountains that contained Glacier National Park. The best thing she could do was hurry and get to her destination.

Her gaze darted to her rearview mirror and then to her side mirrors. Was that a pair of large dark vehicles behind her turning into her driveway? She squinted, but couldn't be sure, and then the distance became too great for her to make out any further details. If she had indeed glimpsed her prospective attackers' arrival, they'd been too late to catch her at home, thanks to Brennan's timely warning.

Tara's mouth set into a grim line, and she pressed harder on the gas pedal. She needed to put as many miles between herself and them as quickly as possible. Hopefully, law enforcement would catch the trespassers before they left her property, but she wasn't holding her breath. Sofie's fussing soon tapered off and ceased. Tara glanced over her shoulder and discovered the child resuming her nap. Driving often seemed to soothe toddlers. What a blessing it would be if she snoozed through the trip.

Tara settled into the prospect of hours on the road. As part of her preparations for a potential emergency departure, she'd kept the Jeep's gas tank full, so she would not need to stop and refuel. Time passed, and after a while, Fairfield had come and gone, then Choteau. The bridge over the Dupuyer and, later, the Two Medicine Rivers passed beneath her tires. At last, they were through Browning, and the route began to climb toward snow-covered peaks that gleamed white in the darkness that was creeping in. Now her headlight beams began picking up snow flurries that quickly thickened into steady snowfall driven by winds that punched at her vehicle with gusty fists. All too suddenly, a blizzard with whiteout conditions and sustained high winds engulfed the Grand Cherokee like an earth-bound tsunami.

Tara's breathing became heavy as the outdoor conditions worsened, and pains shot through her hands from squeezing the steering wheel as she fought to keep the rugged vehicle on the road. Or, at least, what she hoped was the pavement in the middle of the disorienting swirls of white. Occasional slips and slides warned her that the road beneath her tires had grown icy.

The windshield wipers and the defroster struggled to preserve what little visibility remained. Her heart hammered against her ribs in rhythm with the wipers. This early October storm was unexpected, though snow could occur even in September in this mountainous area.

One thing she could be thankful for—the baby slept on. *Please, God, get us to the cabin safely.*

Then, a large darkness appeared in her headlights. Moose! Hitting the animal would kill them all. Well, possibly not the enormous creature.

Tara turned the steering wheel as quickly as she could without jerking the vehicle into a spin on the highway, but her hasty care went unrewarded as the wheels lost traction. The ditch loomed, then consumed them. The Jeep went briefly airborne and then halted suddenly as the front end met the far embankment at the edge of the evergreen forest. Metal screeched and groaned, the rear end bucked against the sudden stop and the driver's side airbag punched Tara's chest and face. Pain fizzed through her body, her head spun, and coughs spasmed her chest from the chalky airbag dust. Sofie wailed in the back seat.

Tara took comfort in the sound. The baby was alive.

For long minutes, Tara fought to still her adrenaline-shaking body, pull adequate oxygen into her lungs and quiet the despair speaking evil things into her inner ear. Yes, they survived the crash, but what were they supposed to do now? They were in a wrecked car in the middle of a blizzard on a winding mountain road that no one would be foolish enough to travel on right now. They could freeze to death before help came. They could—

A knock on the driver's side window yanked Tara's galloping thoughts to a halt. She turned her head, and her world tilted. Just when she was certain the situation couldn't get worse, it had.

Intense hazel eyes set in a masculine face wrapped with a thick reddish beard and mustache peered at her. The face belonged to what seemed to be a large man, probably early to mid-thirties, bundled in winter gear. Check that. A large *armed* man. In the backwash of one twisted headlight, the metallic glint of a rifle barrel winked wickedly at her from the crook of the man's elbow.

A breath hissed into Tara's lungs between her gritted teeth. The baby-snatch squad had caught up to them. Her handgun lay at the top of her go-bag, but she'd never reach it in time to stop whatever violence this man meant to do.

The acrid smell of a hot engine combined with spilled oil tweaked Gabriel McCray's nostrils as his gaze searched the interior of the wrecked Jeep. He identified an attractive woman in her late twenties or early thirties in the driver's seat, with no discernible injuries beneath the airbag powder coating her face and clothes. And was that a baby safety seat in the rear? Yes, definitely. Infant wails carried faintly to his ears over the roar of the storm. What was the woman doing out here with a small child in the middle of a blizzard? Then again, the tempest had come up quickly with little to no weather service warning. Good thing for her and her little tyke that he'd been heading this way, coming down the mountain, and witnessed the accident happen, as well as the hulking cause of the wreck.

Gabe met the woman's stare—more like a glare, actually. Long practice in life-or-death situations had made him fairly adept at reading people's expressions. This woman's gaze held a potent mixture of fear and fury. If her eyes were lasers, he'd be incinerated.

He tried a smile, but the friendly gesture made no apparent impact on the woman. Possibly because he was out of practice with smiling. Maybe she thought he was grimacing or scowling. Huffing through his nose, Gabe lifted a hand and tapped the window with his knuckles.

"Are you okay?" He yelled to be heard over the wind's

howl. The strips of exposed skin above his mustache and around his eyes stung from the icy snowflakes peppering his skin.

A puzzled expression replaced the ferocity in her gaze. Tentatively, she nodded. Her hand moved, and the window opened a crack.

He attempted another smile. “I’m Gabriel McCray with the Park Service.”

“The Park Service?”

Her jaw gaped as if he’d said something astonishing. Maybe she was concussed. Couldn’t she see the patch on his jacket? He glanced down toward his shoulder. Huh! The patch was folded in on itself and not visible from the way he was cradling his rifle. He’d brought the weapon along in case the moose got ornery and charged, but the big guy had moseyed off into the trees while Gabe was making his way down to the wrecked vehicle.

“Your Jeep isn’t going anywhere without a tow. We need to get you and your child into my truck. I can take you somewhere to shelter until the storm passes.”

The woman’s whole body slumped as if relief were a paradoxically heavy weight.

“Thank you. Yes. We would appreciate the lift.” She moved to unbuckle her seat belt. “Can you help me with our things?”

“No problem, ma’am.”

Her gaze sought his. “I’m Tara Markson, and this is my niece, Sofie.” She tilted her head toward the child in the back seat, whose cries had dimmed to hiccupy sniffles.

“Let’s check her out and make sure she’s okay before we move her.”

“Right.” With a groan, the woman turned her body toward the back seat.

"Are you all right?"

"Bumps and bruises, I think, but nothing serious." Her words floated back to him as she reached toward the child and ran her hands over the small body. "I think Sofie is okay, just frightened by the crash."

Something let loose on Gabe's insides, like a fist he hadn't known was squeezing his gut. What a relief the kid wasn't hurt. Not merely because he hated the pain of innocents, but an injured infant would have added a catastrophic complication to the situation in this hostile weather.

"Let's get you folks to my truck." He tried to open the back door, but it was locked. "If you'll open up for me, I'll get Sofie out of her car seat."

A click confirmed that he had obtained access. He opened the door and began unsnapping the belts that had held the child safe during the jolting crash. Large curious dark eyes studied his actions even as the fussing completely ceased. He zipped up the snowsuit that had only been half fastened and tugged the hood over the child's little head. The kid offered him a big toothy grin.

What do you know? She actually seemed to like him, or at least to trust him.

While he was busy, the front door opened, and through his peripheral vision, he noted Tara Markson's cautious emergence into the wind that whipped thick waves of chestnut hair around her face. As Gabe gathered the toddler to his chest, she zipped up her puffy jacket and held out her arms for her niece. He relinquished the child with a surprising nip of reluctance.

Who would believe a doe-eyed kid could grab stone-cold professional ex-Air Force Pararescue Staff Sergeant Gabriel McCray's heart in seconds flat? His team would have scoffed at the notion. If they were still alive. Gabe's insides hardened, and he gritted his teeth.

"Would you grab Sofie's bag?" The woman gestured toward the floor of the rear seat. "I've got mine."

Gabe shook off the mental darkness that had distracted him and returned his attention to the woman before him. A heavy-looking duffel bag hung from the crook of her arm opposite the one cuddling the small snow-suited child. Altogether, Ms. Markson had her hands full and still needed to climb up the steep ditch through snow and ice to reach Gabe's service truck. He'd have to help her.

In preparation, he slung the strap of his rifle over his shoulder, so the weapon hung at his back. Then he gripped the straps of the baby's bag and pulled it out of the Jeep. Turning, he cupped his hand under Ms. Markson's elbow.

"Slow and steady will get us there the quickest and safest." He jerked his chin toward the heavy-duty pickup idling at the far side of the road above them. The storm turned the big object into little more than a black blob.

They faced a climb out of a steep ditch steadily filling with snow that masked the treacherous ice beneath. He took a step in the right direction, but the woman pulled back.

"What?" Gabe whipped his head toward her.

"We'll need Sofie's car seat, too."

He stifled a groan. Of course they would. "Let's get you two into my warm truck, and I'll come back for the seat."

"Fair enough."

Together, they struggled step by step up the grade. Snow pellets whipped exposed skin, and the baby began to whimper. The little girl buried her face in the shoulder of her aunt's puff jacket. The woman stumbled, and Gabe strengthened his grip on her elbow. His Arctic work boots probably had better traction than the more fashionable-looking boots on the woman's feet.

About halfway to their destination, a pair of headlights shot a muted glow through the murk. Great! Another foolhardy driver on the road. Hopefully, they'd take note of his vehicle and exercise caution as they passed. He'd left his lights on, so they should see the extra vehicle on the roadside.

But they were coming too fast.

Gabe's breathing stalled. The last thing they needed was another accident. And it could be bad. If the oncoming car hit his truck, the three of them on foot could be hit by a pinballing vehicle.

Suddenly, the newcomer braked hard, and the vehicle—a large SUV—slewed sideways with a squeal and went into a skid broadside down the road. The woman let out a small scream and hugged her niece with both arms. Gabe tugged the pair behind him, though his presence between the woman and child wouldn't mean much for protection if the SUV plunged into the ditch and hit them.

The skidding vehicle screeched to a rocking halt, still on the road, headlights glaring into Gabe's eyes. Even as he blinked against the snow-slashed brightness, car doors opened and then slammed. A familiar spark accompanied a roar, and something plucked the sleeve of his jacket.

Someone was shooting at them. Who? Why?

He didn't have a split second to spare trying to gather answers to questions. Whirling, he wrapped the woman and child in his arms and sent them into a rolling tumble back down into the ditch, where the only cover might be found behind the battered Jeep.

# TWO

Tara clutched Sofie close as they rolled down the ditch's steep grade, wrapped in the ranger's arms. Her head spun, along with her body, and her niece wailed, the sound muffled against her jacket where the girl's frailty was sandwiched, safe but uncomfortable, between the two adult bodies. No further gunshots followed their whirling progress, but angry shouts from above carried to her. Unless she missed her guess, somebody was getting their ears chewed for opening fire, putting the baby at risk. Given half a chance, Tara would do worse than holler at the careless creep.

The tumbling trio thumped to the bottom of the ditch with their landing softened a bit by the accumulating snow. Ranger McCray sprang immediately to his feet, carrying Tara and Sofie with him willy-nilly. Tara gasped, sucking sleety snowflakes into her throat, as the man thrust them down behind the steaming nose of her Jeep. She coughed, swallowing a verbal protest at the rough treatment. The guy's instincts were spot on. The engine block offered great cover.

Crouching next to her, the ranger unslung the rifle from his shoulder and began to run his hands over it, no doubt checking for damage. Tara had let go of her bag somewhere during their abrupt roll down the hill, or she would be retrieving her own gun. He must have found no problem with his firearm because he brought it to his shoulder and pressed the trigger. The weapon barked, and glass shattered, reducing the headlight glare to a single source.

Tara grinned in involuntary admiration. This guy knew what he was doing. Now their assailants had been warned that their prey was armed and dangerous. The kidnapping crew would have to exercise caution in what they did next. How many guys were up there? Two? Four? Either way, the small group crouched behind the Jeep was outgunned. Or maybe not. Zander's crew would not dare shoot at them again with Sofie present. They would either need to withdraw and leave the snatch for another time or try to flank the armed defenders in the middle of a blizzard. The answer depended on the level of desperation among these guys.

How much pressure was the loathsome father putting on his team to get results? Probably quite a lot. Without his daughter, the man wouldn't allow himself to disappear 100 percent, so the longer Tara kept Sofie from him, the more exposed he continued to be to those who hunted for him. Good for her, but bad for him. That's why this situation created circumstances ripe for continued aggression, despite the risk.

"Give us the kid, and you can go." A masculine shout fought through the storm's howl.

"Not happening!" Tara screamed back.

Bile bit the back of her throat. She'd feel so much better if she had something—no, *someone* to punch. Linnea should still be alive, and her niece should be safe and warm at home with her loving family.

The ranger's head whipped toward her. "This is about the kid?"

"Yeah. The dad's a violent criminal with no custody rights, but he doesn't care about a little thing called the law."

"Was that the dad calling out to us?"

"Nope. The man has fled the country, but he operates fraudulent call centers worldwide, bilking people out of their money 24/7. Finances to hire mercenaries are no challenge to him."

The ranger let out a growl and shook his whole body as if something slimy had touched him. Yeah, that's the way she felt, too.

A gun cracked, and glass shattered. Their assailants had shot out the rear window of her Jeep. Apparently, she'd been mistaken that they wouldn't fire on them while she held the baby. Of course, the bullet had been sent to intentionally miss them. For what reason? Scare tactic?

Rifle remaining at his shoulder, the ranger's body swiveled one way, then the other. "They're trying to keep our attention while one or more of them gets around us."

Tara's hair stood on end. Flanking them, exactly as she'd thought. "I'll keep watch to the right. You take the left."

The man's beard flexed, indicating a nod.

An odd noise began catching her attention. Was that barking? Did the mercs have a dog to send after them? No, the noise came from the far side of the road.

She nudged the ranger in the shoulder. "Is that your dog going nuts up there?"

"No doubt Macky's coming unglued. He hates being left in the truck and missing the action."

Movement to the north grabbed Tara's attention. A mere shadow within the wall of white. A man? An animal? The latter was unlikely with all the shooting going on. An idea came that felt more than a little foolish, but it was all she had. She lowered her fussing niece to rest in the snow, then gathered a fistful of the wet white stuff and packed it into a solid orb the size of a baseball. The cold leached the heat from her bare fingers, and the digits ached, but the warmth of her flesh turned the ball into heavy ice.

A frigid wind blast swept what seemed like a bucket of snow into her face, blurring her vision more than it already was. Beside her, the ranger jerked to attention and sent a round to their south. Someone out there yelped, and action exploded around them. Whoever remained above on the road began unloading bullets into Tara's hapless Jeep. No doubt, trying to distract the ranger and her from the crew members sneaking up on them.

Not working.

The ranger fired again toward the south, even as a dark figure charged in from the north. Gritting her teeth, Tara hurled her ice-ball at the threat. The figure jerked backward and then fell with a shrill cry. The dog's barking suddenly gained volume, as if the animal were no longer inside a vehicle. Snarling mixed with screaming erupted at the roadside, and the gunfire halted. Apparently, the shooter had better things to do than plink at a car when he needed to defend himself from an angry dog.

Abruptly, the attacker who had come at them from the north erupted from his prone position in the snow, turned tail and scrambled up the bank toward the merc's vehicle. Tara bottled a cheer. Way too soon to celebrate.

"They're retreating." The ranger lowered his rifle. "I'd give them more incentive to leave with another bullet, but I might hit Macky." The man lifted himself higher, peering over the Jeep's hood, and hollered his dog's name along with a command to come. If the animal were well-trained, that should bring him right to them.

Car doors slammed, tires screeched and the enemies' vehicle lurched away, the single headlight bobbing along the snow-roughened road. Throaty barking heralded the departure. Then, a large four-legged creature turned and bounded through the snow toward them.

Shaking, Tara scooped up Sofie and cuddled her close, even as the dog slipped and slid the final distance and crashed into his master, who bumped into her and the baby. They all tumbled into the growing snowbank behind them. Dog breath washed over Tara's nostrils from the panting canine who came out on top.

"Off, Macky," the ranger commanded, and the animal retreated.

Tara struggled to her feet, still clinging to Sofie. "Let's gather up our things and get out of here. Those guys will be back, probably with reinforcements."

"Great idea."

The ranger led the way as they both worked to locate the dropped bags. Tara's jaw clenched as she hefted hers. The minute they climbed into the park service vehicle, Tara meant to retrieve her handgun and make sure it was in her jacket pocket, ready for quick access. It had been a mistake to leave it in the bag in the first place. She turned to find the ranger holding Sofie's bag *and* the child's car seat.

With an appreciative nod, Tara began the trudge upward toward the road. The route was slick, and the snow accumulation resisted her progress. To her surprise, the dog took up a post somewhat behind and beside her, lending the weight of his shoulder against her legs to aid her balance for the climb. Smart critter. Gallant, too. So far, she'd discovered that the animal's owner shared the characteristic. How long the selfless service might last after being shot at, Tara couldn't guess. No doubt, the guy would be eager to get Sofie and her off his hands.

At last, they reached the road, and the ranger came up beside Tara as they crossed the icy tarmac toward the truck.

The driver's side rear window gaped wide, indicating where the dog's paw, accidentally or on purpose, had held the button down long enough to open it. Their little group passed in front of the truck, the throaty rumble of its motor competing with the storm's howl. The man started to open the front passenger door, but Tara stopped him with a hand on his arm and then motioned toward the rear. With a nod of understanding, he opened the back door and set the child seat inside.

Tara gently loosened the grip Sofie had taken on her jacket and held her out toward the ranger. They were almost certainly in for another round of wailing from the little girl at being left in the arms of a stranger, but Tara needed to buckle the car seat into place, a task she meant to perform to her own satisfaction. She blinked and stared when the child's fussing, which had started immediately upon separation from her aunt, abruptly ceased as the ranger enfolded the toddler in his big arms.

There was no time to waste marveling at small wonders, so Tara turned away and worked as quickly as her nearly numb fingers allowed, getting the safety seat situated. Then she took Sofie and strapped her in firmly but comfortably, remembering to unzip the snowsuit halfway and lower the hood so the little girl would not overheat once they got going in a warm vehicle. Sofie waved her arms, kicked and vocally protested the operation. Tara spoke firmly but gently to her and finally left her with a sippy cup in her chubby little hands.

At last, Tara climbed into the front passenger seat. Much of the heat had leached from the cab, but the fan was blowing warm air, so the chill would soon be overcome. The ranger let his dog into the rear seat and closed the window. Tara turned her head to find the rust-colored animal with floppy ears settled in tongue-lolling contentment beside

Sofie. Friendly eyes returned her assessing stare, though she'd already witnessed how fierce the animal could be under threat. If Tara wasn't mistaken, the dog was a young, sturdily built redbone coonhound.

Without a word, Ranger McCray climbed inside, and they got on the road.

"We're going the wrong way." She glanced at his furry ice-rimed profile.

"Not to get to my place."

"But I have a destination."

"Right now, it's my place. We're close by, and I'm not driving farther up the mountain in the teeth of this storm. Afterward, we can figure out where you and half-pint need to go."

Tara huffed. "Deal."

"Not a negotiation."

She crossed her arms over her torso and glared at the man. What had ever given her the impression this guy was gallant? He might be brave and a more-than-decent shot. That headlight hadn't been easy to hit in the blurred glare and the swirling snow. But he was rude and stubborn. Why did Sofie seem to like him? Tara was going to talk to that girl about her taste in men.

Too bad the ornery ranger was also correct. In this storm, they had no choice but to adjourn to the closest shelter. Sure, he'd defended them under attack, but that might have been sheer self-preservation. Well, maybe not, since he'd grabbed her and Sofie and protected them with his body during the roll down into the ditch after they came under fire.

Tara bent, unzipped the duffel at her feet and retrieved her gun. A smidgeon of tension unwound from her chest at the solid, reliable weight in her hand. She tucked the weapon into her jacket pocket for ready access, just the way she'd promised herself she would.

The ranger made no comment about her activity. Grim-faced and silent, he stared into the storm. Something deep and heavy bothered this man. Something that might make him unpredictable? Tara intended to be on high alert every moment they spent in this stranger's company. What a predicament. She needed to be wary of the stranger who accompanied them, even while she kept her weapon at the ready for the next attack from ruthless mercenaries.

Gabe capped his inner inferno beneath a thick shield of brooding silence. The incongruous firefight in the middle of a snowstorm on the backside of nowhere had stirred up all sorts of nightmarish thoughts and memories. He was supposed to be done with battle, and yet battle had come to him. Old skills had awakened as if he'd never put any distance between himself and who he used to be.

Then again, if he wasn't still somewhat that person, the outcome of today's exchange of gunfire might have been tragically different. The woman, Tara, handled herself well, too. What background prepared her to move like a pro from a bone-rattling car accident to a firefight—in her case, an ice-ball fight, clever woman—without losing a step? He would ask her about it if he didn't dread issuing an implied invitation for her to question him as well.

Gabe stole a side-eyed glance at his adult passenger. She was hugging herself and huddled inside her jacket. The interior of the cab hadn't warmed up thoroughly yet. But her gaze remained sharp and steady, focused on their slow route down the mountain.

If those guys came back for another run at them, she was prepared. As soon as they got into the truck, she took a handgun from her duffel and put it in her jacket pocket. Her actions suggested a law enforcement background of some kind, but probably not an ex-soldier like himself. She didn't have that indefinable air of military training in her posture and movements. Maybe he no longer did, either, so he probably shouldn't assume anything.

Gabe risked a glance over his shoulder to check on the little girl. Her eyes were wide open, too, like her aunt's, but they focused on the dog lying by her side. Macky seemed equally enraptured as he licked her pudgy outstretched hand. The kid giggled, and the tension in the cab eased.

"We're only a mile or so from my place, Ms. Markson." Gabe's voice emerged with a rusty note, as if he didn't exercise it much.

True reflection of his life these days. By choice, rather than by chance.

"Tara, please." She turned her head toward him and then quickly away. "I'm glad we're close. Sofie probably needs a diaper change by now, and I'm sure she could eat something."

"Me, too. Soup and grilled cheese sound good?"

"That sounds *really* good."

The smile in her voice warmed Gabe's insides as thoroughly as any hot broth. A nice feeling, but not comfortable. It was good to do the right thing for people, but craving approval risked becoming emotionally entangled with others. Unwise.

Gabe slowed the truck, noting the slight ice slippage under the wheels. He slowed further and came up to his turnoff cautiously. After all, he had precious cargo. They wheeled onto the gravel drive leading to his place. The evergreen forest lined the route on either side. His tires crunched through half a foot of heavy snow. No struggle for the sturdy four-wheel-drive.

Then the structures on his property came into view, and he almost winced. A somewhat ramshackle shed tucked up against the tree line sheltered his pride-and-joy personal project. And across the driveway, the garage where he housed his park service truck and outdoor equipment loomed nearly as large as his dwelling. In light of bringing guests home, something he almost never did, the modest A-frame seemed more like a cabin than a house. He and Macky filled it well.

Adding a woman and a baby, with the child's accompanying paraphernalia, might make the space seem cramped, especially since he only had one bedroom. The kid might need to sleep in a makeshift nest made for her on the floor. And the woman? Gabe shrugged. Oh, well. A night in his recliner wouldn't kill him. She could have the bed. They'd manage. It wasn't like he was looking for a guest rating. They'd have to settle for warmth and a reasonable degree of safety.

Gabe activated the garage door opener and pulled the truck in beside his small multipurpose tractor, snowmobile and motorcycle that alternated duty with the seasons.

"Those guys from before won't know where you've gone, Ms. Mark—uh, Tara." He turned to face her. "You can rest here." He didn't add that they needed to report the shooting incident to the county sheriff's office, though there would be no point in sending anyone out here to the scene until the storm passed. With a fugitive involved in the incident, maybe they'd even have to get federal marshals involved, too. "For now, let's get inside."

Tara frowned slightly, probably hearing his unvoiced next step loud and clear. The woman was sharp and had probably already thought the matter through. How she felt about being on the run with an infant because law enforcement apparently was unable to protect them from a criminal hardly needed saying out loud.

The woman nodded and opened her door without a word. Gabe busied himself letting Macky out and grabbing the child's bag while Tara retrieved her niece and her own duffel bag. The interior of the garage might be out of the wind, but still the frosty air nipped his cheeks and the tip of his nose. The temperature had plummeted right before the storm began, with sleet morphing into wet heavy snow, and the air had grown colder. They couldn't be far off from single digits now, and the flakes were lighter but falling much thicker. The wind whistled around the corners of the garage and his house. If he didn't know the month was only October, he'd think the calendar read January.

In a tight group, they hurried to the mudroom entry of his house. Holding the door open, he waited for his guests to step inside, followed by an attentive Macky. Honestly, his dog seemed suddenly to have developed nursemaid tendencies as he sniffed anxiously at the little girl's feet dangling below her aunt's arms.

"Whew! Roll me up and call me a snowball." The woman shook herself and bounced the wiggling bundle in her arms.

Sofie giggled, Macky sneezed and Gabe grinned. Maybe hosting these strangers overnight wouldn't be so bad. Tara apparently had a sense of humor.

"Take off your boots and hang your coats out here, and then come on in." Gabe jerked his head toward the inner door that led to the kitchen. "The place isn't big or fancy, but it's warm, and a blaze in the fireplace will make it cozy."

"Sounds terrific." Tara began shucking her niece and herself free of their winter outerwear.

Divested of the bulky jacket, Gabe noted her trim, athletic figure, which accentuated her above-average height—about five feet eight compared to his six feet two. He showed her the mat that accommodated their wet footwear. Then he opened the inner door to lead them into his compact kitchen, but she lingered in the mudroom, eyeing her jacket beneath a furrowed brow.

"After what we've just been through," he said, "I don't blame you for wanting your gun nearby. We can find a handy place for it out of reach of little fingers. I want to clean my rifle and have it ready, too. But let's leave that until we've settled in and organized."

Her chocolate brown gaze met his, and she gave a decisive nod. "Sounds like a plan. I want to tend to Sofie first."

Gabe decided to put off calling the incident into his headquarters or notifying the sheriff's office until immediate human and canine needs were met. No urgency to report while the storm howled.

The next hour and a half passed quickly as they attended to the toddler's needs, got a fire going in the living room fireplace, fed Sofie and themselves, tended to their firearms and finally settled in front of the cozy fire with mugs of hot tea. Macky snoozed, curled up in his bed near the fireplace, while the baby enjoyed her bedtime bottle and her little eyes grew heavy. Nothing of any consequence had been spoken between the adults during that time. Now, Gabe's stomach tensed as Tara stared at her little niece, and an emotion he readily identified as sorrow drew the lines of her jaw taut beneath high cheekbones.

Would she tell him more details about what happened? Did he want to know? Yes, he did, against his better judgment. Her story might tempt him to become more involved in her situation, and he didn't welcome that. As soon as he had more info, he would definitely call the authorities and leave the situation in their hands.

Tara's expression became cool and calm. Apparently, she would rather not discuss the dire aspects of the situation in her niece's hearing, regardless of whether the little one could understand the words. Gabe respected that, so he would wait until she put the toddler down for the night.

"She's sound asleep." Tara brushed a lock of dark hair off her niece's brow. "Let me put her in the little bed of blankets and pillows we made for her in your bedroom next to where I will sleep. Then I need to call my partner and let him know where we are."

Gabe's heart gave a pang at the word *partner.* Did she mean someone from work or a significant other? Why did he care? He'd just met the woman, and any attraction he felt for her meant nothing and would soon pass. Right?

His guest gathered her sleeping niece close and scooted toward the edge of the sofa. "My partner, Brennan's probably on pins and needles. He'll want to—" Her words halted on a gasp. She turned stricken eyes on Gabe. "I left my phone in the Jeep. It was in the cupholder until the accident. Then I never saw it, never thought of it, until this minute."

Gabe shook his head. "You can use mine. Retrieving a phone will have to wait until the storm dies." As if to punctuate his comment, a sudden blast of wind rattled the windows. "But maybe leaving it behind was for the best. How resourceful is your sister's criminal ex-husband?"

Tara's face blanched. "No. I never… I didn't think… Could he?" She stopped the spate of words and huffed. "I must be in denial. Most crooks don't have the capability to trace cell phone locations, especially when the phone is set up to repel access, as mine is. Law enforcement can't even do it without a court order and the cooperation of telecommunications personnel. But the guy we're talking about isn't your average criminal. He could buy whatever illegal service he needed to track my phone's location. Money is no object for him. No wonder his crew found me in the middle of nowhere in a blizzard. Thank you for bringing this security risk to my attention."

"Security risk?" Gabe scrunched his brows together. "Most folks don't talk in those kinds of terms. You must be in some sort of personal protection business or maybe a cop."

She smirked. "The federal kind of cop. US deputy marshal."

Gabe's mouth formed an *O*. The identification explained her competence under fire. He started to suggest they both reach out to whoever needed to know what happened, but the urgent squawk of his park service land mobile radio cut him off before the first syllable.

The stationary LMR unit sat in his office, but the notification carried up the hallway from there. His boss's voice called Gabe's name over the airwaves, and the tone was urgent. Then again, it usually was, because Gabe served as Glacier National Park's lead search and rescue operator.

Who else was out there in the park at risk in this weather? Whoever it was, Gabe and Macky would need to go help them. It was his job.

His gaze settled on the somber-eyed woman and sleeping child in his living room. If he went out to do his duty and this pair's enemies located them again, they would be left to fend for themselves against an unguessable number of determined assailants.

# THREE

Tara carried Sofie to the bedroom while Gabe hustled into his office and shut the door. She situated her niece in the soft nest of blankets and pillows that her host and she had arranged on the floor by the bed. Sofie was likely out for the night. However, since she'd gone to sleep a bit earlier than her usual bedtime, she'd probably be up at dawn and fussing for breakfast. Tara smiled at the thought. Even her niece's fussing was cute. Then the smile faded.

If only a hungry toddler's cries were the most challenging expectation for tomorrow. There seemed to be no simple solution to their hunted predicament. She sighed. They'd landed in a temporary safe haven, but what were they going to do when the sun rose and the snowstorm ceased? A new day wouldn't bring lifted spirits, but deeper danger.

Sitting back on her haunches, Tara watched her niece sleep. Such an adorable bundle of innocence and trust. How could this inexperienced auntie possibly measure up as a parent, even if bad actors weren't pursuing them?

A great weariness flowed through Tara. She could use some pillow time right now, but first she needed to communicate with her partner at the Marshals Service and brainstorm safety plans. More heads working on the problem might help discover the next viable step for the unwilling fugitives. At least she could be glad that she still had the problem to solve, and the situation hadn't already ended in abrupt disaster out on the highway.

If she were on speaking terms with God, she'd thank Him for sending Gabe around at exactly the right time. While she *might* have gotten herself and Sofie out of the situation with Zander's crew after she went into the ditch, a positive outcome had been much less likely without the park ranger's intervention, not to mention the help of his handsome dog.

She had to admit, Ranger McCray wasn't bad-looking, either. He'd appeared a bit of a hairy wild man, bundled up with only his bearded face showing, his skin reddened by the storm and snow stuck to his eyelashes and thick mustache. Once out of his bulky outerwear, he presented with neatly trimmed, though a bit longish, auburn hair and beard, and a tall sturdy build—not slender, but not husky, either. The man's outdoorsman lifestyle showed in his fitness and the smooth economy of his movements. And those eyes of his… She'd thought them hazel at first glance, but they changed with the light and his mood, sometimes appearing more amber and sometimes more green. Unusual.

Tara shook herself. She had no business mulling over their host's attractive qualities. Personality-wise, he presented as an enigma, waffling between being taciturn, almost to the point of rudeness, and a considerate host who served unexpected guests a hot meal, a fond but firm pet owner and the guy who tickled a toddler in between flipping grilled cheese sandwiches and making her giggle. The smile he'd given Sofie in return had lit his whole face and made Tara gasp at a wave of attraction toward him that nearly swamped her. As soon as she shook off the magnetism, she attributed the phenomenon to an emotional roller coaster of a day.

Now was the time to get a status update from the Marshals Service and make plans for tomorrow. Tara left the bedroom and pulled the door almost closed, leaving an inch or so opening so she would readily hear Sofie if she cried. A glance toward the office door revealed that it remained closed. A murmur of voices carried to her from inside the room, but she could make out none of the words. She would have to wait for him to finish so she could request the use of his cell phone.

Tara returned to the living room and sank onto the sofa. Her tea had grown tepid, but the liquid soothed a tense throat. She stared into the fire, watched the flames dance and let her thoughts drift.

Linnea's familiar lovely face appeared in her mind's eye, skin glowing with health and mouth smiling—the way her sister had looked the last time Tara had seen her alive. After the turbulent patch of learning Zander's true nature, the divorce and giving birth, Linnea had finally landed in a good place mentally and emotionally. She'd found a hotel management job, and Sofie had become the light of her life and a stabilizing influence. Then, Zander's brutal, selfish nature hit like a wrecking ball—stealing, killing, destroying—and the story wasn't over yet.

Tara's fingers curled into fists. Her head fell back against the cushion, and she squeezed her eyes closed. *Oh, no, you don't. You're not getting what you want this time, Mr. Wolf. You are not invading Sofie's life.*

Soft but firm footfalls brought her head up. Gabe reentered the room, his face pale and drawn.

"What?"

He cleared his throat, perched on the edge of an easy

chair, and rested his elbows on his knees. “I don’t know how to tell you this.” He folded his hands together.

“Just tell me.” The words emerged sharper than she’d intended.

Gabe sighed and sat up straight. “That was my boss on the radio. I thought he would be conveying a call-out for me, since I’m the main search and rescue person in the park, but apparently, he wanted to let me know he’d received word from the Marshals Service to be on the lookout for you and Sofie. Earlier today, there was a shoot-out between law enforcement personnel and a crew of armed men in the yard of your home, and neither you nor Sofie were anywhere to be found. Obviously. Lots of people are worried about you, and all agencies are being notified of your disappearance. I—”

“Wait! What? A shoot-out?” Tara’s mouth went dry. “Was anyone hurt?”

Gabe’s dark expression offered no reassurance.

He cleared his throat. “One of the crooks was fatally shot, and a couple of others were injured. Law enforcement didn’t escape unscathed, either. Didn’t you mention your partner’s name as Brennan?”

Tara nodded, unable to get a word out past her constricted airway.

“He was critically wounded.”

“Not—” The word emerged as a squeak. She swallowed deeply. “Not dead?”

Gabe shook his head. “But I don’t have any further information on his status.”

Tara surged to her feet. “I should call headquarters.”

“You cou-ou-ould.” The two words dragged out like the world’s worst drawl.

She fixed him with a steady stare. "But you don't want me to do that."

"Up until a few minutes ago, I would have said yes. But then I did something really dumb, at least career-wise for me."

Tara flopped down onto the sofa cushion. "You didn't tell your boss that Sofie and I are here."

Gabe slowly shook his head. "I had fully intended to report your presence until I heard how badly the situation had blown up because of the high-profile gunfight and the BOLO issued on you and the baby. If I had told him where you were, that information, and possibly your exact location, would have been broadcast to every law enforcement agency in the state and maybe beyond. If this Zander character has the sort of resources you claim, how hard would it be for him to have ears tuned to police band communications?"

Tara's breath hitched. "Not hard at all." She pressed her hand to her lips.

Withholding vital information from his superior could easily land Gabe in hot water regarding his job, but his reticence may have saved Tara's life and Sofie's future. At least for now.

Gabe's expression softened. "If you have someone in your office you could contact privately, I'd suggest you do that. Thc fewer people who know where you are, the better."

Tara inhaled deeply and let it out slowly. "Agreed." Her mind sifted rapidly through data. "At this point, I'm not sure who a safe contact might be. Other than my partner, and that's no longer an option. Let me give you the CliffsNotes version of a horrible story." She smoothed nonexistent wrinkles from her jeans with her palms.

"My older sister, Linnea, had a degree in hospitality

management and had just worked her way into a good promotion with a big company when she met too-suave, overly handsome businessman Zander Wolf in the course of her duties. The guy swept her off her feet and then on to Vegas for a cheesy wedding and glitzy honeymoon, which I knew nothing about until everything was over and done with.

"Linnea fell pregnant almost immediately and was ecstatic. But halfway to her due date, the FBI showed up on the newlywed prospective parents' doorstep with an arrest warrant for Zander, but the guy had skipped the country the day before without notifying his wife. He'd apparently been tipped off by someone somewhere in the legal system about the pending arrest. Needless to say, Linnea was massively confused and intensely depressed while she fended off suspicion and accusations of her involvement in Zander's unsavory activities. Thankfully, I secured her a good lawyer to guide her through the mess, and that lawyer recommended an excellent divorce attorney. Thus, within a single year, my sister was married to a crook, divorced from said crook and a single parent who hadn't been able to hang on to her job during the upheaval.

"Then, Zander decided he wanted his kid but not his wife and took lethal—not legal—action to make his wishes happen. Linnea was getting back on her feet with a new job by then, and I visited frequently to ensure things were on track. But one day, I arrived at her little rental house less than a minute too late to stop a hired killer from stabbing her to death." Tara's throat thickened, and she avoided meeting Gabe's eyes, in case any sympathy reflected in them dissolved her into futile and embarrassing tears.

She cleared her throat and forced herself to continue speaking in an even tone. "I did manage to capture the hired assassin and keep him from taking Sofie. The guy confessed to being hired by Wolf to kill his wife and grab the baby. The judge awarded custody of my niece to me, but that legality means less than nothing to Zander. So, here we are playing keep-away from a maniacal narcissist."

During the course of the story, Gabe had slumped farther and farther into his seat. When Tara finished speaking and met his gaze, he slowly shook his head. "Wow! Yeah, that's…incredibly hard." He sat up and leaned forward. "You mentioned Zander being tipped off by someone within law enforcement. Does that mean you suspect someone inside your own service?"

Tara rippled her shoulders. "The tip-off that sent Zander scurrying out of the country probably originated either within the FBI or in the court system. However, someone with connections to special agents or judicial system officials could easily have tentacles throughout law enforcement, including the Marshals Service. That depth of reach would match the kind of RICO offenses he's charged with. Therefore, since taking a leave of absence from the service to care for my niece, I've been limiting my communication to my partner, whom I implicitly trust. He's the one who called me and warned me Zander's crew was on the way."

"How did he find that out?"

"He said a confidential informant told him."

"Interesting." Gabe stroked his fingers through his ruddy beard. "This Zander character has informants in law enforcement, and law enforcement has at least one informant in tight with the criminal camp."

"That's often how it works."

"I wouldn't know. My service was more straightforward. Get in there, don't get shot or blown up and yank our people out of bad situations by any means necessary."

"Military?"

He nodded with a thin-lipped frown and a touch of that burdened look she'd noticed in the truck. "Air force para-rescue specialist for twelve years. We're sometimes called para-jumpers, hence the nickname PJs."

It was Tara's turn to say "wow," so she did. "That's Special Forces, right?"

He nodded without comment. Tension spread through her middle. She'd been forthright with him about her situation, but he was being guarded about his background. To be fair, though, he was probably legally prohibited from talking about the kind of military operations he'd been involved in. She knew enough to recognize that the thirty-something ex-soldier before her was a very specific breed of dangerous.

More dangerous than Zander Wolf?

Tiny spider feet skittered up her spine, and she shivered as a thought took hold.

Not for her benefit, but for the sake of Sofie's entire future, Tara admitted to herself that she needed help. Something she *hated* to do. With a special operator by her side, maybe she could survive her ruthless adversary long enough for the evil man to be captured and incarcerated. The park service ranger had already risked both his life and career to keep them safe, and he'd consistently treated them with gruff kindness.

What would it take to motivate Gabriel McCray to stay by their side? Would his watchful presence be enough to tip the scales of survival and justice in their favor? But, no, Tara mentally shook herself. Zander Wolf was a manipulator and a conniver. She wasn't going to behave the same way. Linnea was *her* responsibility. Some way, they would survive. If only she knew how.

* * *

Gabe's gut roiled. Quite the toxic situation this woman and her niece found themselves in. *God, surely You don't mean to get me any deeper involved in this mess.*

He'd done his bit, hadn't he? Now, someone else could take over to ensure these people's safety. He was just one guy. He no longer had a team. The federal agencies Tara mingled with sometimes had more teams than they knew what to do with. No, this was not his responsibility.

Then, why was she staring at him like he was her only hope?

Then her gaze shuttered, and she looked away. Gabe allowed himself a mental "whew" and brow swipe. For a minute there, he'd thought she might be going to ask something from him that he no longer had to give. But what was she going to do instead?

"I take it you no longer want to make a phone call?"

Those big dark eyes assessed him. "Not yet. Not sure when. Would you do something for me?"

Gabe's chest tightened. "What?"

"In the morning, would you see if you can find out how my partner is doing? Is he expected to recover? That sort of thing."

Something like a coiled spring let loose inside Gabe. She wasn't asking much of him, except a bit of knowledge. "I can do that. Not sure what anyone will tell me, but I'll nose around like a concerned fellow federal employee."

"Thank you." A degree of tension ebbed from the set of her shoulders. "If you'll drive us there, I'd like to proceed with my original plan of holing up in a remote cabin at the edge of the park that belonged to my maternal grandparents. Just until I figure out what to do next. I will leave my phone in the wrecked Jeep. Without a signal booster, the cabin is unlikely to have cell service anyway."

Gabe frowned. "I don't like you having no way to contact anyone."

"Me, either." She shrugged. "But it is what it is. Sofie and I need to be off-grid."

"I have a pair of professional-grade two-way radio handsets that don't belong to the park service. If I leave one with you, at least you could give me a holler if you need anything or an emergency arises."

"That would be awesome."

Her sudden bright smile nearly bowled Gabe off his seat. *Get a grip, dude.* It's not like they were going on a date. This was business, though of a life-preserving nature, and his involvement was going to be basic. Like she said, just until she figured out what to do next.

"Sounds like we have a plan for tomorrow."

"In that case," she rose, "I'm going to try to get some rest."

"Good night."

She nodded to him while covering a yawn with her hand, then turned and headed for the bedroom.

Gabe looked toward his coonhound, who had lifted his head and was watching him with intense eyes. Macky thumped his tail against his bed cushion.

"I guess it's just you and me for the rest of the evening, same as usual. You like our guests, don't you?"

A confirming tail thump.

"Yeah, me, too." He frowned.

Maybe it would be easier for him to wash his hands of the matter if he weren't so outraged by Tara and Sofie's situation. And the kid had him wrapped around her finger the second she grinned at him. As for the child's aunt? Well, he could probably scoff at the effect of her attractiveness if her courage and intellect didn't exceed her good looks. All the more reason to make them someone else's problem tomorrow. Macky widened his lips in a doggy grin, as if he knew better. Gabe tugged at his beard and glared at his dog as he rose from his chair.

"Let's you and me step outside so you can do your business. Then we'd better hit the hay, too. I have a feeling tomorrow's going to be a doozy of a day."

Gabe woke to a silent house, just like any other morning. The minimal light reaching past the edges of his blinds informed him that the sun had barely peeped over the horizon. A normal time for him to arouse from sleep. But normal stopped right there. He was stretched out in his living room recliner, not his bed, and the abrupt wail of a child broke the silence and reminded him of his houseguests.

And what about the storm? The suggestion of sunlight spoke of a clear day. The wind's howl was conspicuously absent. Now came the digging out from however much white stuff the weather had deposited. His little tractor would get a workout. Speaking of which, he'd better get up and get to it. From rustling sounds and soft murmurs emanating from the bedroom, Tara was up and dealing with her niece.

Gabe had left clean clothes for himself in the bathroom the night before, so he went quickly there and put them on. He headed for the kitchen, intent on locating something to serve for breakfast. Macky was waiting by the door to be let out. Gabe accomplished that and then dug a package of bacon and a carton of eggs out of the refrigerator.

By the time he was setting those items on the counter, a weary-faced Tara had come into the room, holding Sofie.

Aunt and niece were similarly dressed in jeans and sweatshirts. The little girl displayed a grumpy expression and rubbed a fist against her eyes. Outside, Macky barked to be let in, and the child's face transformed to eagerness.

Gabe let out a chuckle as he headed for the door. "Someone has bonded with my dog."

Some of the tiredness lifted from Tara's demeanor, and she smiled. "I'd already begun wondering if I should get her a dog or a cat one day. Now I know she likes animals."

Macky walked into the kitchen, shaking snow from his paws. Gabe bent with a towel he kept ready for that purpose and wiped his dog and floor. The animal trotted over to Tara and Sofie, nostrils flexing as he used his sharpest sense to reinvestigate the pair.

Sofie bounced in her aunt's arms. "Down." She pointed to the floor in front of Macky.

Tara gave a sharp cry that froze Gabe in the process of retrieving a frying pan from his cupboard. "What?"

She blinked glistening eyes at him. "My niece stopped communicating in words after...well, you know."

"So, this is the first thing she's said since then?"

Tara nodded and crouched down with Sofie. The dog snuffled the little girl all over while she giggled and grabbed at his floppy ears. Macky didn't seem to mind a bit. He rewarded the effort with a tongue swipe against her plump cheek that drew a peal of laughter.

Gabe found himself blinking against tears the way Tara had been. *Eat your heart out, Hallmark, for missing this moment.*

The tone of the morning turned upbeat after that encounter, and everyone, including the dog, enjoyed a hearty breakfast. Tara volunteered to do the dishes, and Gabe announced he was going outside to start snow removal from his yard and driveway.

As Gabe put on his warm outerwear in the mudroom, Macky appeared in the interior doorway and canted his head at his master. Gabe shook his head. "No, you stay inside and look after your pet toddler."

The dog snuffled his understanding and disappeared inside, tail wagging.

Chuckling, Gabe ventured out into the tundra-like landscape. The temperature wasn't as cold as yesterday—probably in the lower twenties—but the storm had dumped a good foot of white stuff. His boots sank easily through the top two-thirds, which were fluffy, but crunched through the final third of wet snow and ice. Anyone driving today would need to be careful of the treacherous slickness.

An hour of sitting in the cab of his small tractor with a plow attached saw most of the snow shoveled to the edges of his yard and a clear path drawn to the highway. Road crews were out clearing up after the blizzard. The distant buzz and roar of their activity carried to his ears, but the rural route that went by his house had yet to experience a blade. He'd go inside, grab some hot java and enjoy a little reprieve with his houseguests while they waited for conditions to be ripe for them to move out.

They would need to discuss the accessibility of her cabin. If necessary, he could load his little tractor onto his flatbed trailer. His truck could pull it to the cabin's access road and clear the route to her doorstep. Gabe shook his head. Look at him, volunteering for all kinds of helpfulness. Other than doing his job with everything in him, he'd led an isolated existence for the past three years, dealing with people only when he must.

Gabe went inside, removed his cold-weather clothes and

left them hanging in the mudroom. He entered the kitchen to be greeted by the welcome scent of fresh coffee and the sight of a little girl toddling toward him, leading his dog by the ear…literally. Macky seemed happy with the arrangement. Gabe laughed. He could get used to this.

He could. But he must not.

The deep rumble of an engine disrupted the domestic bliss. Was the county snowplow moving past? The timber of the noise didn't sound right for the massive machine. This sounded more like—a quiver ran through him—a Humvee. He knew well what those sounded like. These days, some folks own the domestic version. Getting through the snow accumulation on the highway would take a heavy-duty vehicle like that.

"Gabe." Tara's sharp-edged call came from the living room. "A Hummer is pulling into your yard."

Hissing in a long breath, he strode out of the kitchen and found Tara peeking outside through a crack between the curtains over his picture window. Expression bleak, she turned her head toward him.

"The windows are dark-tinted, but I may have glimpsed a rifle in the front-seat passenger's arms. I'm reasonably sure we've got unfriendly company."

A video-like flash passed through his imagination—Tara under fire as she flung herself between grinning gunmen and baby Sofie. Gabe went stone-still as ice filled his veins. A familiar dead calm radiated from his core to every limb in his body. Combat-ready. How he hated having to feel that way again. But how he welcomed the knowledge that he just might have the skills to defend his guests successfully.

God willing.

# FOUR

Tara's eyes widened, and her skin prickled as an inner transformation morphed their host from a gruff but kind man who had been warming up to her and Sofie into a hard-eyed creature constructed of granite and iron. However, that chilling stare was not directed at her but toward the outside, as if his gaze could pierce the curtain and reach whomever the pseudo-military vehicle had brought into his yard.

How did she feel about that response to the threat? Warm and safe for Sofie and her, but terrified on behalf of whoever threatened them. Not that they wouldn't deserve anything that halted their attempts to kidnap an innocent child and kill anyone who stood in their way. Tara thought of herself as competent in self-defense, but this Gabe guy was on a whole other level, as he'd demonstrated yesterday in his handling of the attack on them at the car wreck.

All these thoughts chased each other through Tara's mind even as Gabe strode forward and twitched the edge of the curtain aside, peering out without exposing himself. Something like a muted growl left his throat and reached her ears.

"The sun is just right above the tree line to highlight several shadows in the vehicle besides the driver, but they're all sitting there like they're not sure what to do next."

Tara's breath caught. "Maybe they aren't certain Sofie and I are in the house."

"Maybe." Gabe let out a soft grunt. "They could be casing all the homes in the area where your Jeep wrecked. But I don't plan to count on that explanation. I'd like you to take half-pint into the bedroom where you slept and keep her busy and quiet."

"What are you going to do?"

An arctic-white grin parted his beard from his mustache. "Greet our guests with whatever hospitality level they invite with their next actions."

"But—" Tara started to protest banishment to a back bedroom, then she caught herself and bit her lip.

As much as it went against her nature to hide, she had to put Sofie's safety first. If these guys got past Gabe, she would be her niece's last line of defense. But hopefully, she wouldn't have to demonstrate how armed and dangerous she could be. Perhaps these people would leave if they believed the park ranger was alone in the house. Yes, Gabe's plan was best for now.

"All right." She nodded and cast her gaze over the living room for the toddler.

Sofie wasn't present, and neither was Gabe's dog. The tot and Macky had been inseparable this morning. Then, a high-pitched giggle came from the rear of the house. Tara followed the happy chortles to the bedroom where Gabe had directed her.

As she entered the room, Macky's smooth chocolate gaze zeroed in on her where he sat sentinel just inside the doorway. Sofie paid Tara no attention as she gabbled baby talk to a stuffed brightly colored cloth ball with animal figures sewn on it that she manipulated in her pudgy hands. Tara scanned the room. The bed she'd slept in last night remained neatly made, but the pillows and blankets on the floor that had been Sofie's resting place were strewn all over the room, along with every single item from her diaper bag, except for the ball that had captured the little girl's attention. No matter the mess. Sofie was happy, and Tara's heart swelled to see it.

A smile began to spread over her face, but a sudden sharp hammering on the front door froze the expression into a grimace. Macky rose to all fours with a rumbling growl. Sofie jerked in startlement, her little face scrunched up, and her mouth opened in preparation for a wail. Tara swooped in and cuddled the child, shushing her and preempting the outcry.

Whoever these guys were, they couldn't be the sharpest tools in the shed. The knocker had to have slogged through a couple of feet of snow on an un-shoveled sidewalk and up icy steps to reach the front door, instead of proceeding to the garage door that had been cleared of snow. Then again, maybe she was wrong in that assumption. One person could have gone to the front door while the others attempted access through the garage. A chill gripped Tara's chest. How could Gabe alone possibly defend two access points to the house?

At a sharp but soft call from his master, Macky bounded from the room, and the dog's deep-throated barks began to sound from the living room. Still clutching a whimpering Sofie, Tara peeked out from around the doorway to find Gabe's sturdy figure hustling through the kitchen toward the side door, shotgun in hand. Clever man. Whoever stood at the front door had probably sprung a sweat at the vicious sound of the dog, while the master of the house headed off any threat coming from another direction.

Drawing shallow breaths and straining her ears toward

what might be going on outside, Tara withdrew into the bedroom and shut the door. Keeping Sofie calm and quiet was her most challenging job right now. Their first line of defense was to deescalate any offensive action by their unwelcome visitors by convincing them that their targets were not present. If hostile ears overheard any baby noises from inside the house, that strategy would be compromised, and things could escalate quickly into a violent situation.

Tara bounced the toddler and whisper-sang in her shell-like ears even as she opened the closet door and her gaze found the butt of her loaded handgun that she'd placed for safekeeping on a shelf far above a toddler's reach. If the worst happened, and an assault began, she would lay the child down, grab the weapon and prepare to use it. The action would further alarm an already agitated Sofie, but at that point, the toddler's wails wouldn't matter. They'd be in a fight for their lives and Sofie's future well-being.

Macky's ferocious barking subsided to a menacing growl, and men's gruff voices rose atop it like an echoing rumble. Gabe had engaged their visitors in communication, but how tense the situation had become was impossible to tell. At least they weren't shouting at each other. That had to be a positive sign, didn't it?

Tara's nervous tension must have been apparent to Sofie, because the little girl continued to whine and wiggle. Tara needed to settle herself down to comfort her niece. She hauled in a deep cleansing breath and let it out slowly, willing herself to relax.

Sofie stopped whimpering and patted Tara on the cheek. "Num-num." The little girl's big eyes conveyed hopeful expectation.

Tara grinned, her heart melting at this continued evidence that her niece's verbal communication had resumed to some degree. "Snack time, is it?"

She knelt and set Sofie down on a blanket. With a little rooting around among the diaper-bag items strewn across the floor, Tara located a bag of cheese crisps. At the sight of the package, the toddler clapped her hands. Tara opened the bag and handed it to Sofie, who immediately dived into the goodies.

Reasonably certain now that her niece was happily occupied, Tara rose to her feet and moved to the closed door. Holding her breath, she listened. Silence met her ears, but not the comforting sort of quiet. More like the weighty lull before the tempest. Or was that an impression fed by her stretched-taut nerves?

A throaty roar rent the silence, and a shiver rippled through Tara's body from head to toe. She hurried toward the gun in the closet. Had that been Gabe's shotgun or the report from one of their adversaries' weapons? Tara's fingers closed around the butt of her pistol, but then she went still, her own breathing loud in her ears. No, that had not been a gunshot, but the angry rev of an oversized engine. The roar had subsided into a low growl, and the growl was steadily diminishing.

Could the best-case scenario be true? The Humvee was leaving?

Footfalls sounded on the floor outside the bedroom, along with the click of doggy nails. A soft knock on the door released Tara from her temporary paralysis.

"Gabe? Is that you?"

A slight chuckle answered her. "Unless Macky has developed knuckles on his paws, I'd say it's me."

Relief flooding her system, Tara snorted and rolled her eyes. She crossed the room in a few strides and opened the door. Macky shot past her legs and went to Sofie, who greeted him with happy chortles. Tara glanced over her shoulder to find her niece offering the dog a piece of her snack. The animal sat on his haunches and received the treat with an air of polite delicacy.

Shaking her head, Tara returned her attention to Gabe. He stood on the threshold, bundled in his heavy jacket with a knitted cap on his head. His figure radiated coldness from the time he had spent outside, dealing with their unwelcome visitors. The chill had painted his broad forehead and the tops of his cheeks, visible above his beard, with a rosy hue. Apparently, he'd returned his shotgun to the holder above the fireplace because he no longer held it in his hands.

Tension ebbed from Tara's body, and her shoulders dipped as she released a huff. "They went away."

"For now."

The clipped tone and residual hardness in his stare returned Tara to a state of high alert.

"Tell me."

"There were four of them, but only two got out of the vehicle. One came to the front and knocked. I sicced Macky on him. By the time I got outside, another one was approaching the garage door. The door-knocker held a 1911 Browning semiautomatic, but it was lowered by his side as if he were trying to semi-conceal it from whoever answered the door. The garage guy's right hand was buried in his jacket pocket, where I assume his pistol was hidden. At the sight of my shotgun, garage-guy pulled his hand out of his pocket, spread his arms from his body as if trying to appear unthreatening, and sent door-dude a sharp glance. The guy responded by pocketing his gun and mirroring his buddy's stance. They both offered wooden grins, like the false-friendliness actually hurt their faces. I asked what their business was, and the garage guy spun me some tale about finding an empty car in the ditch and wanting to report it to the nearest park ranger. They were concerned about whoever had been in the vehicle, and did I know if the person or persons were all right."

A sour taste spread through Tara's mouth. At least one of Zander's mercenaries possessed a modicum of good sense and subtlety, which might be more dangerous than the blunt hammer approach from the attack last night. "How did you respond?"

Gabe smirked. "Told them I'd received no reports about a car in the ditch. Then, I gave them kudos for their Good Samaritan instincts and promised I'd check the situation out."

"Did they believe you?"

"Doubt it, but they left. Sort of in a huff, though. They made a big deal about roaring their engine before ripping out of here as only that beast of a vehicle can do on snow and ice."

"They'll be back." Tara's jaw firmed, certain of her deduction.

"Almost certainly, but I think they'll use stealth this time. Probably tonight."

"We need to get out of here." Her heart tripped over itself. "But how? They'll be watching."

Gabe lifted a forestalling hand. "We can't stop them from watching, but we can control what they see."

"Okay?" Her response was tentative, but she wasn't going to rest Sofie's safety on any half-baked plan.

"I told those guys I was going to check out their report of an abandoned car, so that's what I'll do…in my plow tractor. Once I remove the spare gas can from the cab, there's just enough room on the floor to squeeze in you and half-pint. Cormac sits next to me on a small jump seat, so the watchers will see him through the window and know he's with me."

"Who's Cormac?"

"That's Macky's proper name." A genuine grin split his face as a warm twinkle in Gabe's eyes fully displaced the dangerous glint.

Tara's heart gave an extra *kabump* but she ruthlessly dowsed the spurt of attraction. "Do you think they'll break in here to search the place if they see you've gone?"

Gabe shrugged. "Either that, or they'll follow us. However, my sense is that they'll do the latter. At least, that's what I would do. If their search of the house comes up bust, as it will, they'll figure the Humvee will have little trouble catching up to a slow-moving tractor."

"And when they *do* catch up to the tractor?" Tara planted her hands on her hips and glared at her host.

He grinned bigger. "You won't be with me."

Tara curbed an impulse to punch him in the shoulder. The situation was serious, and this guy seemed to switch from Terminator-style cyborg to *Tombstone*'s flippantly menacing Doc Holliday in the blink of an eye. The guy even looked a little like Val Kilmer might if he'd had a full beard and red hair.

"Explain," she gritted between clenched teeth.

"No time." He shook his head and turned away. "Pack up. It's time to move out." He threw that last sentence over his shoulder as he strode away toward his office.

Tara clenched her fists at her sides. Next time, she might not resist the urge to sock him. Maybe this guy had ordered people in the military, but this wasn't the army, and she wasn't his grunt. Nevertheless, gathering their belongings and leaving no trace that a baby had ever been in this house seemed like a wise move. Sighing, Tara turned away from the door and got busy.

Twenty minutes later, her and Sofie's bags were stowed behind the seat in the small tractor, and she was hunkered on the floor of the fuel-and-dust-smelling cab like a pretzel squeezed into a very small space beside the driver's seat with a bundled-up Sofie clutched in her arms. Thankfully, the toddler had decided it was time to take a nap and was already falling asleep. The child's stillness dialed down the physical discomfort to bearable levels. Not so much the mental and emotional stress.

As the tractor trundled slowly up the driveway toward the paved road, grim knowledge pressed in upon her like an ever-tightening vice. She and the most precious thing in the universe to her, other than God Himself, who she was currently mad at, were now heading *toward* the danger lurking on the highway and not away from it.

Would Gabe's strategy work and see them safely away? Or was a trap about to clamp iron-toothed jaws around them?

As they approached the end of his driveway and the entrance to the paved road, a surge of pain in his hands alerted Gabe that his fingers were clenching the tractor's steering wheel like a tether to life itself. *Chill, dude.* At his self-admonishment, his hands eased their grip, and the pain went away. He wouldn't be doing Tara and half-pint any good if he stayed wound up like a spring ready to bust. What happened to his ingrained ice-man response to pressure?

He glanced down at the woman huddled on the floor and the precious sleeping bundle she held. Therein lay the problem. Staying frosty when working side by side with his military colleagues, both men and women, had never been an issue, but providing close, personal protection for an infant was entirely new territory. The responsibility got on his last PTSD nerve. Yet, deep down, he couldn't escape the impression this was an assignment from God, and therefore a privilege. *God, help me.*

Gabe stopped the tractor at the edge of the turnoff onto the road with one side graded free of snow by a county plow he'd heard pass by while they were getting ready to leave his house.

"Everyone okay down there?" His voice emerged with a hoarse edge from the tension still knotting his insides.

"We're good." The soft but clipped response from Tara let him know she, too, was wound tight.

Gabe swiveled his head from side to side as anyone would do in search of oncoming traffic before pulling out, but more to see if he could spot any watchers. The coast appeared clear, but he didn't trust appearances. These people were too determined to get what they wanted for anything to be made easy for their quarry. Macky's head also turned from one side to another, his eyes wide, and his posture stiff and tall on the jump seat beside Gabe.

He let out a soft chuckle. "You're on high alert, too, eh, boy?" A muted *whoof* answered him as the dog continued to look this way and that.

"Here we go, then." Gabe eased the tractor into the turn and out onto the plowed side of the barren road.

No one would be proceeding very fast over the thin slick of ice and snow that frosted the pavement. With the temps still well below freezing, the treacherous coating wouldn't be melting away anytime soon. That circumstance could work in their favor, slowing their adversaries down and limiting their access where roads and driveways remained clogged. Gabe was counting on the conditions as an ally in keeping Tara and Sofie safe. So far, so good.

Or not.

As the tractor chugged up the road, Gabe's peripheral vision caught the barest glimpse of a vehicle's snout poking out of the tree line in what looked like a poorly and hastily hand-shoveled turnaround. If he weren't mistaken, the front grill on the vehicle was missing a headlight. Though the forest hid most of the vehicle, he got the impression of an SUV, not a Humvee. It didn't require a great leap of deduction to suspect the SUV was the same one that had contained the attackers from last night.

"We have watchers," he murmured to Tara without glancing down at her or looking directly toward the ill-hidden vehicle. Gabe held the tractor steady on the road, no slowing down, no speeding up. "Not the Hummer people, but the SUV folks."

A small snort answered him from Tara. "Zander's got incredible reach. I'm sure he has multiple teams blanketing the area. Our attackers last night would have noted your official park service vehicle at the crash site. No doubt every park ranger in the area is receiving a visit from concerned citizens reporting a car in the ditch, hoping to initiate a telltale reaction from whoever might be hiding the people they want to find. Is the SUV following us?"

"Not yet. I figure they'll either do that or wait until we're over the hill and out of sight. Then they'll scoot on over to my place and search it."

"Probably the latter."

"I think so, too. How certain are you that every evidence of your presence was erased?"

"Totally. I even looked under the bed for any item Sofie

might have flung there, and I thoroughly wiped down the bathroom of any trace of presence other than yours."

"Good enough. I made sure they'll find only one set of dishes in the dishwasher."

Tara let out a sound like a cross between a growl and a snarl. "I hate that your privacy is being invaded by these creeps."

Gabe snickered. "If the activity keeps armed and dangerous manhunters out of our hair, then I wish them a nice long engagement in a fruitless activity."

"Good attitude." She huffed a sigh. "So, where are we going?"

"My neighbor's place first. I promised to clear out her driveway this winter. She's a recent widow who wants to sell her homestead in the spring and move closer to her grandchildren, but for now, she's alone out here."

"I don't want to endanger anyone else."

"No worries. I'm not dropping you off there."

"Then where?" Impatience and tight-strung nerves bled into her tone.

"My place. When we get back there."

"What?!"

At the sudden outburst, a mewl came from Sofie.

Gabe grinned and glanced down where Tara had begun rocking the little girl back to sleep.

"Pretty clever, huh? Hiding you in a location that has already been searched."

"All right." She snickered. "You win the Sneaky Award. How long do Sofie and I have to hunker down here? My leg is cramping."

Gabe frowned. "I'm afraid it will be at least another hour."

Tara grunted and squirmed into what he hoped was a

more comfortable position. "Better that than risk my niece being taken."

"I agree, but I'm sorry for the discomfort. I have to clear out my neighbor's yard to lend the appearance of a normal snow-cleanup day, and then do what I told those mercenaries I was going to do—check out your abandoned vehicle. Only then can we return to my home. Hopefully avoiding further surveillance."

Tara tapped his leg, and he met her upturned gaze. "Would you be able to retrieve my phone from the car and Sofie's stuffed bear? She hasn't seemed to miss Teddy since she's been fascinated with your dog, but I don't know how long that reprieve will last."

"I suppose I can get into the car through one of the shattered windows." Gabe furrowed his brow.

"You shouldn't have to go through those contortions. The key fob got left in the front cupholder when we fought and fled last night. The door should open right up."

"Hmm." Gabe considered the issue. "Okay. That might work. Assuming I will be under surveillance when I access the vehicle, I'll make a point of ducking inside and coming out with the fob in plain sight. Anyone watching will understand that the vehicle was open. Then I can act like I'm searching the interior—glove box, back seat, et cetera—for clues about the owner. I'll tuck the phone and the teddy under my coat. However, we're going to have to immediately disable tracking on the phone and shut it off."

"How about this instead? Hide the teddy, since you would have no reason to remove it from the car, but openly take the phone like you're going to use it for potential contact information or in case someone calls the number, and you can find out who it belongs to."

"Clever." A smirk formed on Gabe's face. "The bad guys

will then assume the tracking information is useless to them, since the phone is in the possession of a meddling park ranger and not its rightful owner."

Less than an hour later, the neighbor's driveway had been cleared, and their operation at Tara's abandoned vehicle had gone off without a hitch. If he said so himself, Gabe had put on a stellar performance with the key fob, as well as the phone. A glint of sunlight reflecting off glass or metal from a nearby hillside informed him that he had indeed been under surveillance from some no-doubt miserable watcher hunkered down in the cold.

But as he'd returned to the idling tractor on the side of the road, a shiver had run down his spine at the sudden realization that the glint may not have been from something as benign as binoculars. Maybe it had been a riflescope. If the person collecting the phone—and the bear—had been Tara, she might not have survived the moment. When he returned to the driver's seat and left the scene, he'd kept that thought to himself. Now, as the tractor chugged over the top of the last hill before his place, a knot began to loosen inside him. Almost home free.

Then the roar of an engine behind them stiffened Gabe's spine. A monster vehicle shot over the crest of the hill behind them, going entirely too fast for the conditions, even though it was a Humvee with wide tires.

"Incoming!" Gabe reached up and grabbed the shotgun that had been resting in the overhead rack.

Tara's gun, which had been tucked into the back of Gabe's waistband for safekeeping out of Sofie's reach, slid away from his back as the US deputy marshal retrieved it.

"How sure are you they're after us?" she called out as her niece awoke with a startled cry and began to fuss.

The tractor's rearview mirror showed the massive vehicle chewing up the yards between it and the tractor. Seconds before the Hummer would have rammed their back end, the vehicle swept wide around them into unplowed territory, blowing waves of white powder and fishtailing on the ice, then roared ahead. Hope spurted that they had not been the target after all, but then the reckless creature in the driver's seat must have slammed on the brakes.

The Hummer whipped a sliding turn that whirled the vehicle 360 degrees and then some, finally coming to rest side-on, blocking traffic. Blocking *them*. Four hulking menaces brandishing automatic weapons sprang through open doors and set up firing stances in their direction.

Gabe brought the tractor to a halt in the middle of the road. The *put-put-put* of the diesel engine marked time, like an eerie metronome, in the sudden, ominous inertia.

"Oh, I'm very certain they're after us. One hundred percent."

# FIVE

"What's going on?" Tara's voice came out thin and sharp. Her heart flailed against her rib cage as Macky began to growl.

"The Humvee is blocking the road, and all four occupants are pointing guns at us."

"Why? They have no reason to go after you. I don't get it."

"Me, either. Something must have given them the idea I know where you are, or that you might be with me."

"Maybe we missed something telltale at the house, and the searchers called these guys to stop us."

Gabe grunted. "Makes the most sense of any explanation." His jacket sleeve brushed the top of Tara's head as he reached for his phone in a holder on the dashboard. "I'm going to call for help, though I doubt we have enough time for it to arrive."

While he spoke to someone, Tara anchored her gun, still with the safety on, underneath one of her legs and bounced Sofie to quiet her, but with poor success. The little girl was awake and unhappy, and no one was going to fix that in a hurry.

Gabe finished his call, receiving a promise of backup

within the next fifteen to twenty minutes. Not soon enough by any stretch of the imagination.

Tara tapped his leg. “Give me the bear.”

“The b—? Oh.” He pulled the teddy from inside his jacket and passed it down to her.

With a happy squeal, Sofie hugged the soft toy and stopped fussing.

“What are the Hummer guys doing?”

“Still standing there, pointing guns at us.”

“I think they’ve painted themselves into a corner and don’t know what their next step should be.” Tara released a bitter chuckle. “They don’t dare shoot at the tractor because Sofie might be in here, but they can’t let us get away, either.”

“Okay. One of them, probably the leader of this odd squad, is motioning for me to get out of the cab.”

“Are you going to?”

“Not on your life.” Gabe did something with the shifter, and the tractor began to creep backward.

The sharp report of a gunshot, followed by the whine of a ricochet, sent Tara’s heart into her throat and wrung a startled cry from Sofie.

“Those dirty creeps!” Tara snarled through gritted teeth. “I can’t believe they shot at us.”

“They didn’t. It was a warning plink on the pavement.”

The tractor continued to roll slowly backward up thc hill. Tara folded her fingers around her pistol butt and prayed the heavy tires wouldn’t slip against the ice and snow. And that the slimeballs from the Humvee wouldn’t continue to fire their weapons.

A bass rumble from behind them grabbed Tara’s attention. What now? Another Humvee?

Gabe’s head swiveled to look over his shoulder. “It’s the

county plow on its way back down the mountain, clearing the other side of the road."

A doubling of the decibels punctuated his words, and seconds later, the shadow of the county behemoth cast shade over the tractor windows as the machine crept past them in the other lane.

"What are the Humvee guys doing?" Tara raised her voice to be heard over the racket.

"Piling into their vehicle and peeling out." Gabe let out a brief chuckle. "Mr. Snowplow can squash Mr. Hummer any day of the week."

"What are we going to do now? We can't go back to your place. The SUV crew may still be there waiting for us if they found something that indicates Sofie and I were there."

In response, their tractor rolled forward and changed lanes. "I'm going to fall in behind the plow and follow it all the way to the county garage. I don't think you have any choice, now, but to call your people and get protective custody. There must be someone you trust to make the arrangements discreetly."

"You're right." Tara scowled. "The time has come for you to hand us off to the Marshals Service. You've already gone above and beyond anything you should have been expected to do."

"If I thought I could keep you and Sofie safe on my own, I would."

"I know."

She didn't doubt a word of his pledge. He'd already demonstrated on their behalf the sort of courage and competence that must have made him an excellent Special Forces operator. And his pararescue specialty flagged an off-the-charts instinct to protect. Strangely enough, though she'd only met him yesterday, her gut preference would be to trust him rather than her own service, but that option was no longer practical since his involvement with her was apparently known to the enemy.

"Hand me your phone, would you? Mine is still too frozen to attempt using it."

Tara accepted the cell phone from Gabe. Heart heavy, nerves raw, she tapped in the number for her direct boss in the Great Falls, Montana, office of the Marshals Service. As much as she dreaded officially giving away her position, at least she could ask how her partner, Brennan, was doing after he was injured in the shoot-out at her place.

"US Marshals Office, Great Falls, Montana. Henderson speaking. I don't recognize this number."

Her boss's words were clipped and semi-aggressive. He was probably shocked to be called on his direct line by an unknown number.

"It's me. How's Brennan?"

Silence answered for the length of a heartbeat, then Henderson let out a gust of breath. "Tara?" The question emerged in a muted bellow. "Where are you? Are you and Sofie all right? We need to get you into protection."

"We're fine." She squirmed a little in her cramped position on the floor. Here was the moment of truth—letting people know where to come collect her. Of course, since the enemy already had a read on her general vicinity, she wasn't letting loose much new information. "I'm with a ranger serving in Glacier National Park. We're on our way to—" she looked up at Gabe "—where did you say we were going?"

Those enigmatic hazel eyes glanced down at her, and he rattled off an address. Tara repeated the information to her boss.

"It's the garage where the county keeps its big equipment. We've had a winter blast up here."

Henderson humphed. "We got some here, too, but nothing like up there. Okay, I'll get a chopper in the air to come get you."

"A helo?"

"Yes, it would take too long overland with the roads the way they are."

"I appreciate that, but you never answered me about Brennan's condition."

"We don't know yet." Henderson let out a heavy sigh. "He was life-flighted to Billings, where they've got top neurosurgeons. A team there removed a bullet from his head. Even if he lives, no one—not even the docs—can predict how well he'll come back from that. They're keeping him in a coma until the brain swelling goes down. Then, we'll see."

Tara's stomach churned. Her friend and partner had taken that bullet for her and for Sofie.

She swallowed against a dry throat. "How long for the transport?"

"Anywhere from an hour to an hour and a half, depending on how fast I can get the arrangements made and the pilot can spool up the bird. You going to be all right at the location until then?"

Tara looked up at her driver, and he met her gaze, no doubt easily overhearing Henderson's end of the conversation. Her boss didn't exactly have a quiet voice.

Gabe nodded. "I'll stay close with the shotgun until they pick you up."

"That the park ranger?" Henderson's tone went guarded.

"That's him."

Tara's boss huffed. "He may be a federal employee, but

he's not law enforcement, and this is no longer the Wild West."

"You could have fooled me." Tara's words held a sharp edge. "The way outlaw bullets have been flying near a baby out here. Besides, he's an ex-Air Force PJ. Knows how to handle himself under hostile fire. I'd trust him any day of the week."

"Okay. Okay." The tone was placatory. "I didn't realize you'd come under fire. That makes it even more critical to get you out of there in a hurry."

"You'll have a full report when Sofie and I are safe."

"I'll make it happen as quickly as I can. Is this the number I should call when the chopper is on the way?"

"Yes, I'm not sure when mine will be operational again. It froze."

"Why do I figure that's another hair-raising story for later? All right. I'll keep you posted."

They ended the call, and Tara returned the phone to Gabe's waiting hand. He quickly used it to place another call, informing people at the county that they were coming in behind the plow and needed to pull his tractor into a garage bay out of sight. Tara appreciated the bare bones but complete explanation he provided for the unusual circumstance. Just enough to let them know the situation was critical, but not immediately dangerous.

Then again, Tara told herself, it didn't pay to assume safety. "Any sign of a Humvee or an SUV with a broken headlight?"

"Nada. We'll tuck the tractor away and hide out in a back room until the bird arrives."

"Sounds good. I can hardly wait to get off this floor, and Sofie needs a diaper change and a meal."

To punctuate the seriousness of the situation, the little girl began to fuss.

Gabe's low chuckle warmed the cab. "I think we can arrange that. We're pulling into the lot now."

Their park ranger protector was true to his word. Tara never saw the locality they pulled into or the outside of the building that encompassed the cavernous space filled with massive machines where Gabe parked his tractor, but within five minutes, she was wriggling her way onto her feet and passing a still mewling Sofie down into the park ranger's waiting arms. Even as her half-asleep legs prickled with pins-and-needles sensations, their little group was escorted by a county employee from the chilly fuel-smelling garage into a utilitarian back office where warmth embraced them, along with a mild, scorched coffee aroma.

A round-bellied man with a wind-burned face and friendly blue eyes offered a steaming cup of the brew, which Tara gladly accepted. The man introduced as Bob, the head of county road maintenance, went into another room with Gabe, and Tara could make out the soft rumble of their voices but no words. The ex-PJ was no doubt filling Bob in on the situation. How would he and his staff react? Gabe had assured her they wouldn't back down an inch, and they all carried and knew how to use what they had—mostly .22 rifles and a few handguns.

Sighing, she set her mug on a nearby desk and tended to Sofie's needs, including a diaper change and a pre-packaged toddler meal. Not Tara's usual choice for feeding her niece, but the situation called for emergency-style rations. Nearby, Macky perched, tongue lolling, his watchful gaze fixed on the toddler. When Tara spread a blanket from Sofie's bag on the floor and sat Sofie on it with a bag of dessert treats, the dog settled down on his belly beside her and planted his head on his paws, though his eyes stayed wide open. The toddler welcomed the animal's presence with a tug on one of Macky's ears. Tara bottled a chuckle.

With the little girl entertained, she checked her pistol over, making sure it was ready for use and well out of a child's reach. Now they just had to wait, which was sometimes the most challenging part. She was under no illusion that they were home free or safe in this location. Sure, Gabe and the personnel who worked here stood between her and the ruthless people who were after Sofie, but that also meant they were in danger, too, and there was nothing she could do to mitigate the risk—other than giving up her niece, but that wasn't an option.

With her pistol within arm's reach, Tara sat in the chair behind the desk, swiveling slowly back and forth while Sofie finished her treat, played with her bear and teased the patient dog. A soft knock at the door sent Tara's hand reaching for the weapon, but Gabe stepped through and wagged his phone at her.

"Henderson."

Tara leaped up and took the device. "Are we on with the helicopter?"

"Should be landing behind the county building in fifteen minutes. Be ready to hop in and take off immediately."

"You remember I have an infant with me?"

"Absolutely. A child seat is installed."

"Excellent. We'll be ready."

The call ended, and Tara handed the phone back to its owner with a heartfelt thank-you. She owed him way more than a few words, but it was all she had at the moment.

Gabe nodded in acknowledgment. "You might want to

leave your cell with me. I've still got it in my pocket. It's plenty warmed up now, but if the evil ex's minions have a lock on its signal…well." He shrugged.

"Take a hammer to it."

"Will do." He grinned, and Tara's heart gave that irritating jump his smile seemed to evoke.

How had she ever thought this guy was cold and humorless?

"Keep watch over half-pint." He nodded toward the happy toddler. "I'm going to do a swing around the premises, then come back for you when the chopper arrives."

More minutes passed while Tara ensured that all their belongings were ready to go. At last, a distant *thump-thump-thump* carried to her ears. Pulse quickening, she put Sofie back into her warm snowsuit, much to the child's displeasure. Macky rose to all fours and didn't look happy, either. But Tara was hopeful for the first time in a long time. Maybe they would get out of here and be whisked to parts unknown without being attacked.

As she zipped up Sofie's outerwear, a gunshot pierced the noise of the helicopter's engine. The bird sounded as if it were directly overhead, but the gun blast came from inside the building. Then came the sharp crack of a .22 rifle. She'd know that distinctive sound anywhere.

Tara tucked Sofie under the desk, and the dog came and stood at the opening. Watching. Guarding.

She snatched her pistol up and moved toward the door, only to jump back at a sharp knock, followed by a command in a familiar voice to hold fire. Gabe burst into the room, shotgun in hand, and that scary yet comforting ice-machine expression on his face.

"Despicable Daddy's trigger-happy mercs are here. They must have had eyes on us as we followed the snowplow to the garage." He motioned with his shotgun barrel toward the door. "We've got seconds to get you and half-pint to that chopper."

Keeping his head on a swivel and his shotgun ready, Gabe ushered Tara and her precious cargo up the hallway toward the rear exit. From the noise up ahead, the chopper must be landing in the rear lot. Behind them, toward the front of the building, more gunfire blasted.

Battle calm enveloped him even as furnace heat smoldered at his core. These criminal minions needed to be shut down and locked away, along with their boss. They were probably shocked at the pushback from the county maintenance crew resisting their kidnapping attempt, but these mercs must have forgotten they were dealing with Montanans. Carrying guns and knowing how to use them were part of the culture. Still, a prayer went up from his heart that none of the brave county employees would be hurt.

As their small group neared the back exit, the gunfire suddenly ceased while the chopper's thunder wound down, indicating the bird had landed. In the comparative silence, the click of Macky's nails against the scuffed tile floor and the toddler's resentful mewling gained volume.

Tara reached for the door handle, but Gabe laid a hand on her shoulder. "Let me peek out first."

Expression grim, she nodded and pressed her back against one wall. Her sharp gaze studied the environment behind them. One hand gripped her pistol down at her side. The other arm clutched her niece close with the child's bag dangling from her elbow.

Gabe stepped past her and cautiously opened the door. No gunfire greeted him. A small four-person blue-and-white US Marshals Service helicopter, blades still lazily whirling, sat about ten yards from their location. A uniformed deputy marshal armed with a rifle hopped out of the front passenger door and took up a defensive position, gaze and gun scanning the open area. The pilot, still in his seat, motioned for them to dash across the open area.

Gabe moved outside and waved Tara toward the chopper. She hustled past him toward the little bird awaiting them with the potential of a flight toward safety. Gabe followed in her wake, head on a swivel. About halfway across the open area, she staggered over a slick spot on the tarmac. He reached out to steady her just as a rifle report cracked from the far edge of the building.

Clearly, the mercs had figured out the action was in the rear parking lot, and now the opportunity for escape balanced on a pin's tip. The deputy on guard returned fire. Gabe swept Tara and Sofie close, putting his body between them and the aggressors. The pilot responded to the urgency by hopping out and opening the rear door to allow quick access for the evacuees.

Gabe quickened the pace. Only a few yards to go, and he could get them into the helicopter. Surely, the mercenaries would hesitate to shoot the bird once their precious quarry was inside. Once they were secure, he'd join the deputy marshal on the ground in battling the mercs while the pilot got Tara and Sofie away.

Solid plan but doomed in a heartbeat by a stray bullet that ricocheted off the pavement and struck the pilot as he attempted to return to the cockpit. The man cried out and collapsed to the snow-packed ground, writhing and clutching his side. The defending US deputy marshal moved in closer to his downed compatriot, continuing to fire at the mercenaries who hid around the corner of the building.

Three county employees burst out the rear door of the facility and joined the suppressive fire.

"We need to get back into the building," the deputy hollered.

Gabe shook his head. "You get the injured pilot to safety. I'll fly Tara and Sofie out of here."

The deputy's jaw opened as if he would protest, but then he jerked a nod. "Go!"

Needing no urging, Tara dove into the rear of the helicopter and began buckling Sofie into her seat. Macky leaped through the pilot's open door and hopped up onto the copilot's seat even as Gabe settled into the pilot's spot. His gaze devoured the controls, understanding the configuration in an instant and getting his hands and feet working. In seconds, the bird surged skyward.

Below, gunfire had become sporadic. The attackers had lost their quarry and would be retreating. Again. But they might not avoid apprehension this time. Gabe's glance earthward spotted multiple law enforcement vehicles, lights blazing, converging on the county garage.

Then they left the battlefield behind and swept toward the vast pine and evergreen forest blanketing the mountainside. Gabe kept the skids only a few yards above the trees as they moved away from civilization and into the wilderness.

Behind him, Tara's harsh, panting breaths competed with Sofie's frightened wails and the beat of the chopper rotors. Macky slinked his sinuous body between the front bucket seats and joined his passengers in the rear. Moments later, Sofie's crying turned to watery giggles, probably because Macky was licking her face and letting the toddler play with his floppy ears.

Soon, Tara's heavy breathing settled, and she let out a

groan. "Thank you for getting us out of there. Your air force training came in handy today."

Gabe spurted a chuckle. "Ironically, I didn't learn to fly in the Air Force. PJs don't receive flight training. We're all about search and rescue in the most challenging environments—mountains, deserts, oceans and even Arctic locations. I learned to fly on my own time after joining the park service. Pilots could sometimes be in short supply, so I thought it might come in handy to know how."

"Good call."

"Amen."

"Where are we going?"

"Where would you like to go?"

"Anywhere that no one is shooting at us or trying to take Sofie."

"I'm sure the Marshals Service will radio us soon with the coordinates of a safe house."

"What if the bad guys overhear the radio transmission? Zander has massive resources. I'm not sure the safe house will be that safe."

Gabe frowned. "You need to go dark—completely disappear—until a certain nasty piece of work gets taken out of commission."

"Wrong. *We* need to disappear. They'll come after you, because they will think you know where I am. You're not any safer than Sofie and I are."

"I can take care of myself."

"No question. I'm competent in the self-defense arena, too, if I had just myself to think about. But with my niece dependent on me for every bit of care, my focus is necessarily divided. We need you with us."

Tara's words struck Gabe like a fist to the solar plexus. The last time anyone had said those words to him, everyone except himself had died, and he'd nearly joined them. There had been times during his lengthy recovery that he'd wished he had. That the tragic circumstances were beyond his control was beside the point. He was alive, they weren't, and he'd nearly lost his sanity coping with the loss.

His job of search and rescue with the park service often called on him to undertake risky operations. He was trained and highly skilled at the job. But going in and bringing strangers out of dire situations, or even finding some no longer among the living, wasn't the same thing as volunteering for what amounted to personal protection duty for people he'd begun to care about deeply. Failing Sofie and Tara would cost him his soul. Could he really take that risk? But, then again, if he didn't and the Marshals Service failed, as they had been doing so far, how could he live with himself then?

# SIX

Tara gnawed at her lower lip. Where could they go to escape? The question echoed in her heart. Hadn't someone in the Psalms cried out with that very problem? Only the Psalmist had been speaking about escaping God and ultimately concluded that no escape existed nor was desired. The knowledge of God's perpetual presence ministered comfort. In this case, the question of escape from aggressors simply rang hollow…hopeless. Unless—

"Take us to the hospital in Great Falls." She leaned forward and continued to speak loudly so none of her words were swallowed by the rotor noise. "There's a helipad, but I don't want to use it in case a medical emergency is coming in. This bird is small enough to set down in the parking lot."

Gabe glanced back at her, brow furrowed. "That move will create quite a noticeable ruckus."

"Maybe so. Temporarily. My best friend works in the hospital business office. She'll lend us her car in a heartbeat, and we'll drive away in a vehicle no one knows about."

"Driving in a vehicle no one knows about is a great idea, but showing up where you will be recognized and borrowing your friend's car may paint a target on her back. How about this instead?"

Tara's stomach lurched as the helicopter halted and

hovered, then began to lower toward the ground. Her jaw dropped open as they came to rest in the empty yard in front of Gabe's A-frame house.

"We're right back where we started!"

"Not for long." Gabe unbuckled his seat belt and swiveled his upper body toward her. "The GPS in this bird will lead your service, as well as any bad guys who didn't get shot or arrested at the county garage, to this location—one that's already known. But before anyone can get here, we'll be in the wind."

"What? We're going to grow wings rather than rotors?"

He pursed his lips with a gleam in his eyes that Tara could only describe as mischievous. She narrowed hers at him. What was this guy up to?

"In a manner of speaking, you're right." He hopped out of the helicopter onto the snow-packed earth. "Grab half-pint and we'll be on our way."

Biting back protests over the mystery, Tara released Sofie's infant seat from the helicopter, but left her niece buckled in. Whatever vehicle they entered next, the little girl would need to stay in the safety seat. Macky trotted alongside Tara as she followed Gabe toward the scruffy shed at the corner of the property.

Her enigmatic host pulled a key from his pocket and released a padlock from the shed's double doors. Then he pulled one half and then the other half open wide. The sunlight sparkling on the new snow revealed what lay within the shadows. Tara's jaw dropped while Gabe grinned like a proud papa.

Tara snapped her teeth together and cleared her throat. "What is it?"

"A car."

"Yes, I see that, but then again, I've never seen one like it."

"You're not likely to, either, outside of classic car shows." He walked into the shed, trailing a hand down the wide black stripe that ran along the sleek side of the gleaming apple-red vehicle. "And look, there are wings." Gabe stopped and turned toward her, cupping his hand over one of the graceful raised half-arcs that bracketed the long car's massive trunk space. "This is a 1959 Dodge Custom Royal Lancer Super D-500 sedan. My dad—and I, whenever I had leave from the military—restored this baby from near-junk."

"It's a…it's…" Tara scrambled for the right words to express her combination of admiration for the beautiful restoration job and dismay at the thought of taking the vehicle on a road trip.

"It's a beast, right?"

"A beast. Exactly."

"And she runs like a top."

"But—"

Gabe lifted a forestalling hand. "I know what you're going to say. A flashy car like this will draw attention. But that's the beauty of the situation. Would this Zander character or any of his hirelings ever for a moment consider their quarry might be riding around in something like this?"

"No." Tara shook her head. "No, they wouldn't." She could hardly imagine such a wild idea herself. "But you're a known associate with me now. If Zander's hacker people hunt online for any vehicles registered to you, our retro cover will be blown."

At her words, Gabe's smile dimmed, and his gaze went shadowed. Tara almost wished she hadn't had to burst his bubble like that. He was proud of the car, and rightly so.

He shook his head. "They won't find a classic '59 Dodge

registered to me. I inherited this car from my dad when he passed away suddenly from a brain aneurysm three months ago, and I haven't found the time to do the change of ownership paperwork."

"Oh." Lame response, but this new wrinkle in the situation threw her off stride. Then the still-fresh pain on Gabe's face registered with her. "I'm so sorry for your loss." She meant the words, cliché as they were.

Gabe seemed to accept her sincerity, and the dark tension eased from his expression. "Why don't you buckle Sofie in while I grab some supplies from inside the house?"

"I can do that. But somewhere along the route, wherever we go, we'll need to stop and pick up a few clothes for me and more diapers and food for Sofie. I have her bag, but it's getting lighter, and mine got left behind at the county garage."

"No problem." He jerked a nod. "But let's put some miles under the tires first."

Gabe crunched away across the yard toward the house, and she followed his sturdy figure with her gaze. Then Sofie squealed and wriggled, swaying the car seat on Tara's arm.

She looked down, smiled at the little girl and tickled her under the chin. "All right, sweetie. Let's get ready for this epic road trip."

Tara stepped into the shed and opened the rear door of the classic car, amazed at the smooth, soundless swivel of the hinges when something this old might be expected to exhibit joint creaks. The interior was pristine and smelled almost like new, as if it had just come off the showroom floor in 1959. The red vinyl bench seat gleamed, matching the exterior color but with silver-gray insets, where a person's bottom and back would go.

Furrowing her brow, Tara leaned inside with her precious cargo. Would a vehicle this old have seat belts meeting current safety requirements? She released a pent-up breath as she situated the car seat mid-bench. Yes, this noble Royal Lancer did. Perhaps the restoration had included contemporary updates.

Now, looking more closely at the upholstery, fine age lines became apparent, like a gracefully aging human being, exhibiting only a feathering of character wrinkles in the corners of their eyes. Gabe and his dad had done a superb job at the restoration. But then, Gabe had amply demonstrated that he had exacting standards for anything he undertook.

Thus far, she and Sofie had been the beneficiaries of his expertise many times over, and apparently, they would continue to enjoy it. For now, they needed him. At least, he hadn't left them yet and didn't seem to have any plans to do so now that handing her off to the Marshals Service had failed spectacularly. The thought of all those bullets flying outside the county garage jolted Tara. Zander's criminal troops were getting more desperate and therefore more careless, even firing on people when Sofie was nearby. Tara sent up a mental prayer that the wounded helicopter pilot would be all right and that no one else had been injured…or worse.

If fleeing from one fraught situation to the next was her life now, how long would Gabe stick around? She shouldn't expect him to do so. Maybe once he got them far away into an obscure location, she could hunker down with Sofie. Then Gabe could return to his life.

Yes, that would be for the best. Not only was it unfair to expect this near stranger to upend his world indefinitely, but Tara had learned from bitter experience not to rely completely on anyone else. Everyone always left. Always.

Even if the leaving wasn't their fault, like her sister's murder and her parents' accident.

Sure, she needed and welcomed Gabe's help for now, but in long-term reality, she and Sofie were on their own. Tara needed to make peace with that truth, and that meant no emotional attachments—especially not to a too-attractive and fascinatingly enigmatic ex-pararescue operator. She needed to protect Sofie—her niece's safety was paramount—but she also needed to protect herself from any silly ideas that Gabe's care for them could mean anything personal.

Firming her jaw, Tara retrieved Sofie's beloved teddy from the diaper bag and handed it to the squirming toddler. Then she shooed a waiting Macky into the back seat beside Sofie, closed the door and marched around to the front passenger side of the car. Her resolve firmed as she climbed into the seat that embraced her with chilly arms.

She would afford Gabe heartfelt gratitude for all he had done and was doing, along with a measure of trust, but she would not allow herself to become attached or dependent on his presence. After all, they would be parting ways soon enough.

Gabe cast a brief glance toward the woman in the passenger seat. Tara's gaze seemed focused ahead, her face impassive, her posture soldier-straight. They'd been on the road for nearly two hours, traveling steadily southward into flatlands that had seen significantly less snow. She'd been quiet the whole time. If her eyes weren't wide open, he would have guessed she'd gone to sleep like Sofie and his dog. Not that he'd begrudge her a nap. They'd been through a lot, and the day was barely half over.

His stomach was telling him they needed to stop for

a bite to eat soon. Maybe when Sofie let them know she was awake.

"How are you holding up?"

His side-eye caught a ripple of reaction through her body that indicated she'd heard his question. She didn't answer right away, just looked toward him and then returned her gaze forward.

At last, she huffed. "I feel a bit like a hamster in a wheel, always in motion but never arriving at a destination—at least a safe destination."

"I understand your frustration, even though I've only tasted a little of what you've been going through."

Her shoulders visibly relaxed from their rigidity. "I know you do, and I don't expect you to carry on with us much longer. Deposit us somewhere and get back to your life. You must be AWOL from work. I hope your boss is understanding."

Gabe let out a brief chuckle. "Actually, I'm off duty for the next week. There's an annual classic car show this weekend in Provo, Utah, that my dad loved because it's small and intimate. He had lots of pals there that he was eager to see every year. Since he'd already registered for the show, I've been planning to attend in his honor." He offered Tara a smile that felt more like a slightly sappy grimace. "With the show supervisor's permission, I kept the registration in my dad's name."

Her countenance softened. "So, neglecting to transfer the car's title was more on purpose than accidental."

He shrugged. "Call it nostalgic procrastination."

"Then nobody will be missing you at work. But if unfriendly forces question your coworkers, won't they be able to tell them where you've gone?"

"Nope and nope. I applied for vacation properly, but the

form did not include a space for an explanation or destination, so I didn't provide one. My colleagues at work are unaware that I've got the Lancer. That's my business, and this is a deeply personal trip."

"A memorial." Tara nodded, her gaze tender. "Sofie and I are intruding on your special time. I'm sorry about that."

"Not at all. I'm just thankful that my road trip dovetails with the main mission of keeping you and Sofie safe."

"I appreciate the sentiment, and *I'm* glad you're still going to be able to attend the car show your dad loved. I hope our presence doesn't endanger anyone."

Gabe pursed his lips and shrugged. "Right now, either the remnants of Mr. Wolf's crew are attempting to pull themselves together again, or they're all enjoying jail hospitality, and Wolfie will need to hire new people. That's all going to take time. Plus, I don't see how they could have a read on our location anymore."

"What about your phone? They're aware of you as an associate of mine."

"Left my cell on the counter at home. We are officially off the grid." Gabe lifted his hands and waved empty palms, then returned his grip to the wheel. "And, as you can see," he nodded toward the dashboard, "this vintage vehicle offers no GPS or other digital devices to hack into. Just an old-fashioned radio with contemporary top-of-the-line speakers hidden behind the original dash. Would you like to listen to music?"

"Sure." Her acquiescence sounded tentative.

Gabe laughed. "Worried about my taste in music?"

"Not really." A smirk formed on her lips. "In this vehicle, I would guess the choice of repertoire is oldies, oldies or oldies, and I have no problem with that."

He flicked the knob on the radio, and Danny & the Juniors came through rocking "At the Hop." The mood in the car lightened immediately. Gabe turned the volume down so as not to disturb the sleepers in the back seat, yet allowed the adults to enjoy the music.

"This is good." Tara bobbed her head to the beat. "Say, I just thought of something. Why are we *driving* the old car to the show? Don't people usually trailer them?"

Gabe shook his head. "For this show, everyone arrives driving their classic wheels. All year, the people who attend—more of a car family get-together, really—look forward to taking their babies on the road."

"If the circumstances were better, I could almost say I'm looking forward to the trip." She scrubbed her hands against her pants either in a gesture of self-comfort or gearing herself up to introduce an uncomfortable topic. "From the way you talk about your work colleagues, it doesn't seem like you are friends with any of them."

"I wouldn't say that." His words came out a bit clipped. "They're work friends. Well, acquaintances anyway. I like them all well enough, but unless we're stationed at headquarters, we rangers pretty much work on our own out there."

Where was she going with this thought? Gabe's stomach clenched. Already, the conversation had explored personal territory for him. He'd freely shared about his most recent pain and loss. But if this were an intro to moving deeper into history, which covered his final mission in the military, he wasn't going there. Since his honorable discharge with a chest full of unwanted medals, he hasn't spoken to anyone about that dark time—not even his father before he passed away. But then, maybe he's thinking defensively for no reason.

"So-o-o." She drawled the word. "You don't have anyone close enough to you that they might be at risk because you're helping me?"

Gabe's insides relaxed. "Not since my dad passed, and my mom has been gone for many years. Cancer. And I don't have siblings." He forcefully clamped his lips shut against the sudden, startling pressure on his mental dam that blocked the names of his lost team from tumbling out.

What was up with that almost spillover? Why did something in him want to go against his resolve to keep tragedy close, walled away from the world that wouldn't understand? He shot a side-eye at Tara. This woman was dangerous in ways she didn't even know about.

At that moment, Frank Sinatra's "Under My Skin" began playing. Gabe's pulse jolted.

If his unexpected impulse to spill his guts told him anything, Tara Markson might be getting under his skin—or at least slipping around his armor. He couldn't let that happen. He wouldn't.

He'd help these two get to a place of safety, and then he'd go back to his own safe life. Emotionally safe, that is. His search and rescue job required personal risk, but to his way of thinking, physical danger didn't matter compared to risking his heart in caring deeply for anyone. If that made him a *cold fish* or a *loner*—words he'd heard people speak about him—then so be it. Life had stripped so much away from him already. He wasn't going to be foolish enough to set himself up for more loss.

Gabe glanced toward the lovely profile of the woman sitting next to him and then over his shoulder toward the sleeping toddler. A wonderful, terrifying warmth gathered in his middle, along with fierce protectiveness. Unless it was already too late to guard his heart.

As he steeled his jaw and tightened his grip on the steering wheel, the latest golden oldie on the radio ended, and the announcer came on.

"Greetings, hipsters. Got your groove on yet? Whether you're toolin' around in those boss wheels of yours or sittin' comfy in your cool pad tuned in to the radio, we've got a treat comin' up for you." The man's raspy tone conveyed a fair impression of Wolfman Jack, the iconic 1960s DJ. "Here's a special request song from a daddy who's missin' his daughter. And he's got a few words to say to intro the tune. Give a listen. Your heart is gonna break."

A slight click suggested the DJ was either opening the line to someone else or starting a recording. "Hey, Baby Sofie."

This voice was the antithesis of rough. Every syllable emerged sleek and smooth as ermine fur. Yet, a chill ran down Gabe's spine despite the warm tone. This guy couldn't be talking to *their* Sofie, could he?

"Your papa's looking for you every day," the voice purred on. "I'll never give up on you. We'll be together soon. I promise."

Was Gabe imagining it, or did the final two words come out tinged with threat—like a fist in a velvet glove?

He glanced toward his front-seat passenger. Tara's face had gone paper-white, and her hands lay fisted in her lap.

"Was that—"

"Yes-s-s." The answer hissed between thinned lips. "Zander Wolf."

Then The Duprees began to croon their 1962 hit. Most listeners would find the whole father-missing-daughter scenario sweet and charming. But the hairs on the back of Gabe's neck prickled to attention as the doo-wop quintet sang the title words over and over and over: "You Belong to Me."

# SEVEN

Nausea squeezed Tara's middle. She swallowed against it, her throat clicking with dryness. "He knows what…radio station we're listening to. He must know…about your car… where we're going… I can't lose Sofie… I can't—"

"He doesn't, and you won't."

Gabe's firm declarations cut off Tara's words that had been spurting between hyperventilating gasps.

She glared at him. "What other explanation can there be for airing *this* particular message at *this* particular time in *this* particular way?"

"Okay, consider this." Gabe's tone conveyed a steadiness that soothed the flutters in Tara's chest. "His people lost us at the county garage, and I'm sure the abandoned helicopter has been reported found empty by now, so as far as he's concerned, we're in the wind. But it's a rather straightforward deduction for him to figure we've gotten wheels from somewhere. We're traveling. You told me the guy runs international call centers. What's to stop him from tasking a whole bunch of his people to call every radio station in Montana and the contiguous states with requests to air songs appropriate for each type of station, along with the same eerie recorded message from him? He's trying to alarm us into making a mistake."

Tara sucked in a deep breath and let it out slowly. "The effort still seems extraordinary, and if I didn't know what kind of person Zander is, I wouldn't believe it. But this kind of psychological torture would give him great delight. Just imagining us listening to his message has got to be giving him goosebumps. And I have to admit he has succeeded in rattling me, but we don't dare make a mistake as a result."

"Agreed. The best thing for us to do is to continue our journey calmly. Sure, we'll attract attention from classic car buffs along the route, but even if Zander's people spot the Lancer, they are going to follow their instincts and automatically dismiss this vehicle as a possible transport for their targets."

A snicker left Tara's lips. "It'll be a *whodathunkit* moment. Their eyes will skim right across us."

"Exactly. They'll never entertain the notion and keep looking for ordinary vehicles."

An abrupt wail from the back seat interrupted the conversation.

Tara grinned at Gabe and shook her head. "I think someone is hungry."

"More than one someone." He rubbed his stomach. "Good thing there's a big truck stop with a restaurant a few miles ahead, where we hook up with Interstate 15 that will take us all the way to Provo."

Within twenty minutes, they were digging into their food amidst a noisy lunch crowd that kept the waitstaff hopping. The restaurant sported country-themed decorations, the furniture was worn and the carpet was faded, but everything was clean. Further, the personnel were cheerful, and people seemed to be enjoying their meals, which provided a positive testimonial in itself. The place exuded down-home comfort.

Nevertheless, Tara struggled to relax. She didn't want to be hypervigilant, but she was, despite Gabe's calming words in the car. For the hundredth time, her gaze swept over the customers and staff in the truck stop restaurant, and then she studied the parking lot outside the window by the table where their little trio sat. Nobody seemed to be paying excessive attention to them, and no vehicles appeared to contain suspicious characters eyeing the building. Then again, the parking lot was vast. Who knew if a vehicle full of bad actors lurked in a far corner?

Across from her, Gabe cleared his throat, and she met his gaze. Did the slight wrinkling of the crow's feet bracketing his eyes indicate amusement?

"It's okay to eat your food." He nodded toward her full plate. "No one here is waiting to pounce on us."

She let out a pent-up breath and looked toward her niece. Kicking her little feet in the high chair where she sat, Sofie seemed delighted to eat her macaroni and cheese with her fingers, making a mess of her face and hands, and even leaving traces of sauce in her hair.

Tara chuckled and picked up her patty melt. "I've been on alert for so long—well before having to flee my house—that I've forgotten how to wind down."

"I can hardly blame you, considering what you've been through with the loss of your sister and assuming care for your niece, while a creepy ex hovers in the wings like a melodrama villain."

She swallowed the bite of her savory sandwich. "Melodrama? That seems a flippant description."

"What's been happening has been deadly serious. Obviously. But that cheap trick on the radio was pure theater."

Tara nodded as she patted a little grease from her lips with a paper napkin. "The past couple of days, you've experienced the threat firsthand. Zander is completely ruthless. However, I agree with you about the radio thing, but such a stunt is not at all out of character."

"How so?" Gabe took a bite out of his burger, but his gaze remained fixed on her.

Tara leaned toward him. "Here's what you need to understand about Zander Wolf. He's a flamboyant guy. Thrives on attention. Works overtime to charm people. Loves drawing in acolytes like some giant sparkly sun, sucking little planets into its orbit. That's all my sister, Linnea, was to him, another object to reflect his light, and that is what Sofie is to him also. He wants to possess and control her and will stop at nothing to make that happen. Nurturing is not in his nature. Sofie will not thrive with him, and I will not let him have her, even if I must run and hide or fight and flee for the rest of my life."

Gabe's eyes narrowed. "Sounds like something needs to be done to render that lifestyle unnecessary. Sofie deserves stability. You both do."

"I agree." Tara flung her napkin down. "But I have no control over how quickly or even *if* Zander will be apprehended. He's hidden himself away in the Maldives, a non-extradition country." Acid bit at her stomach, stealing her appetite. "Even if US law enforcement could pinpoint exactly where he is in the Maldives, we have no authority to apprehend him, and in-country law enforcement will do nothing."

Frowning, Gabe returned to his meal, gaze focused on his plate like his attention had been captured by his French fries. Tara had the impression he'd gone deep into his head somewhere and was eating on autopilot. Her indigestion flare subsided, and she attempted more nibbles on her sandwich. She needed to keep her body fueled. Over the past few months, she'd lost over ten pounds due to stress. For the same reason, Sofie hadn't been eating and growing the way she should. Tara swallowed a surge of anger along with a bite of her sandwich.

*Why, Lord?* Why did the wicked get away with persecuting innocents like her sweet little niece? Days and nights—especially nights—of fruitlessly casting around in her head and heart for the answer to that question had fastened a stranglehold around her relationship with God, reducing her prayers to resentful, angry and wounded outcries or else cold silence. Her struggling faith added to the list of damages Zander had done to her life.

"We should get going."

Gabe's words drew Tara out of her dark musing. She nodded and turned toward Sofie, who was no longer eating but now only playing with the remnants of her food.

Tara chuckled wryly. "Let's take you to the ladies' room and get you cleaned up, peanut." She stood and began releasing her niece from the high chair.

Across from her, Gabe rose and pushed his chair in. "While you do that, I'll take care of the bill, then go outside and let Macky out of the car to do his business before we get back on the road."

"Sounds good." Tara cuddled her niece as close as she dared without getting gooey cheese all over her own clothes.

Gabe walked toward the front of the restaurant, while she headed to the rear, child and ever-present diaper bag in tow. Cleaning Sofie took longer than she'd intended, what with wiping down hands and face, as well as hair, with wet cloths. The toddler hadn't particularly liked the process and made her protests known. Then Tara had to change her niece's soiled clothes and diaper. Finally, she put the toddler's snowsuit on her, keeping the hood down and the front unzipped. The temperatures were considerably warmer here in the lowlands than in the mountains.

At last, they were on their way out of the eating establishment. Gabe had parked his Lancer around the side of the building in a spot away from other vehicles. She didn't blame him for wanting to do whatever possible to avoid dings on the beautiful bodywork of the vintage car. Tara carried Sofie up the sidewalk next to the restaurant, her gaze involuntarily searching the area for threats, but finding none. The tiniest niggle of relief made its way from her brain to her gut. Then she rounded the corner of the building and froze in place, her heart thumping against her ribs.

Gabe stood with his back to the Lancer's grill, a trio of men positioned in a strategic half-ring confronting him. From inside the Dodge, Macky began barking fiercely while the former PJ seemed to coil into a fighting stance.

Gabe stood in front of his car, knees flexed, arms by his side yet slightly away from his body, poised for action, whatever form that needed to take. Especially now that he'd spotted Tara and Sofie nearby. Wisely, Tara had stopped her approach and appeared to be assessing the situation. However, to keep these aggressive people from noticing her and Sofie, he didn't turn his head in their direction. If he could shoo these people off without involving her, that would be for the best.

Of the three men ranged in a semicircle facing him, the two on the sides looked to be in their late thirties. They were dressed similarly in puff jackets, jeans and scuffed trainers. With heavy jowls and thick necks, the pair displayed bulk in their arms and legs like weight lifters. However, they had begun to sag in the middle, as if they hadn't been keeping up with their diet and training, or they enjoyed their beer too much and no longer cared about their physiques so long as they maintained enough size to intimidate others. Off-duty nightclub bouncers past their prime? Or maybe they were bodyguards to the flashy-dressed forty-something guy between them.

The exceptionally tall, reed-slender man in the center wore an expensive suit with no winter jacket over it, a designer watch, an expensive haircut and shiny shoes. This guy and his bookend minions had been ogling his car when he came up behind them from walking Macky. He'd let the dog into the back seat and then inserted himself between the trio and his Lancer. Immediately, the slick dresser had bubbled over with faux friendliness, offering an eager handshake and a shark smile, while introducing himself in so many words as Lix—short for Felix—Frazier. But Gabe mentally dubbed him the Pencil and his buddies the Erasers. The Erasers maintained their patented scowls while Pencil kept on talking, saying the same things—alternately cajoling and threatening—and jabbing a skinny finger toward the Lancer he coveted for his vaunted collection.

"No. Sorry." *Not Sorry.* Gabe uttered the words for at least the third time in the frustrating non-discussion. "My classic car is not for sale."

"Oh, c'mon." Pencil extended his hands, palms up. "You don't really mean that. Everything's got its price. Uh-huh." The man's pointy chin bobbed as he agreed with himself.

"Hi, honey." Tara's cheerful voice sent a startled ripple through the Erasers, who swiveled their heads in tandem. "I see your car has drawn admirers."

Pencil turned to face the newcomer, toothy smile in place. "You must be the missus. Maybe you can talk some sense into this guy." He jerked his head toward Gabe.

Tara remained on the sidewalk and did not approach the

group gathered on the tarmac. Gabe nodded his approval of keeping her distance. Pencil wasn't so smart. He took a step toward Tara and Sofie.

"Stay away from her." Gabe's words came out with a growl worthy of his dog upon spying a rodent.

"Okay. Okay. Uh-huh." The man halted, his head swiveling between Gabe and Tara. "How about a hundred-thousand? That's above market. You won't make easier or better money. Better grab it and run." His gaze stalled on Tara. "That'll buy a lot of diapers, huh? Take you and the mister on a great vacation. Start a college fund for the kid. What do you say?"

Tara's eyes narrowed, while Gabe tensed himself for swift action if any of the trio closed in on her.

"I say you step away from the car and let us leave in peace." Her voice rang loud and clear. "Or I'm going to scream my head off. This is a busy truck stop. Do you want that kind of attention? Maybe even the cops coming around?"

Color flooded Pencil's face, and his bony fingers clenched into fists. Then Mr. Lix Frazier appeared to rein himself in, and the tension ebbed from his posture. Gabe swallowed a chuckle. He'd been prepared to get physical. Tara's way was better.

"Okay. Okay. Uh-huh." Pencil repeated what appeared to be his favorite phrase. "Let's keep it cool. Can't blame a guy for looking to make an acquisition when he sees what he wants. Here." The man pulled a card from his suit jacket pocket and extended it to Gabe.

Gabe curled his lip like he'd been offered a rattlesnake.

"Take it." Pencil waggled the rectangle of cardstock. "Call me if you change your mind."

He snatched the item. Accepting the business card seemed to be the quickest way to get these people to leave.

Pencil backed up a few steps, ice-blue gaze shooting lasers from Gabe to Tara and back again. Then he whirled on the heels of his shiny shoes and stalked away. The Erasers fell into step behind their boss like a pair of oversized ducklings.

Gabe let out a pent-up breath as his gaze followed the trio to a snow-white Lincoln Town Car. Pencil climbed into the rear seat while the Erasers squeezed their bulks into the front bucket seats. The car glided toward the exit onto the freeway, then suddenly revved and laid a patch of rubber as it sped away in the same direction Gabe's little group needed to go. He narrowed his eyes. One thing was for sure: he was going to be watching ahead for any ambush these yahoos might want to try.

"I have a bad feeling that guy isn't going to give up that easily."

Tara's voice at his elbow drew his attention off the highway and onto her tense face.

"We think the same way."

She frowned. "Is there an alternate route to where we're going? I mean, I know the interstate is faster, but—"

Gabe offered her a lopsided smile. "In keeping with the retro vibe of our journey, I happen to have a paper map in the glove compartment. Let me give Macky a drink of water while you go old-school and plot us a leisurely meander."

She chuckled. "How about we settle for the quickest way to where we're going without driving the freeway?"

With a nod of mutual understanding, they set about their assignments, and soon Gabe had them on the interstate heading toward an exit that would take them off the beaten path without delaying their arrival at the car show by more than a few hours. In the back seat, Sofie chattered unintelligibly to her teddy and her gently panting canine buddy. Alongside Gabe, Tara continued to study the map.

"Huh! Interesting!" she exclaimed at last. "There is a whole bunch of information on a paper map that is not shown on a Google route."

"You mean like topographical details and names of things not plotted on the streamlined digital shot from here to there?"

"Exactly. You can view the entire state on one page and see how things relate to one another. Speaking of names. Did you get one from that lanky creep who wanted this car?"

Gabe dug the unwanted business card out of his pocket and handed it to her. Tara looked at it and gasped.

"What?" He glanced toward his passenger.

She met his gaze with a fierce scowl. "Do you have any idea who Felix Frazier is?"

"No." He shrugged. "Should I?"

"He's a wealthy businessman."

"I gathered that much."

She lifted an admonishing palm in his direction. "He owns notorious nightclubs scattered across the northwestern states."

Gabe grunted. "No doubt where he acquired the Erasers."

"The what?"

"Not what, who. Those two muscleheads he had with him. You know—big, square, spongy in the middle, and designed to correct or eliminate the Pencil's mistakes. Long, lanky Frazier is the Pencil."

Tara spluttered and then burst out laughing. A few heartbeats later, Gabe joined her. Soon, Sofie chimed in with high-pitched giggles, clearly not caring whether she understood the reason for the hilarity or not. Macky enhanced the mood with a few happy *woofs*. All too soon, though, the laughter faded away. Gabe couldn't speak for anyone else, but the belly laugh had lightened a heaviness that had settled in his middle since finding Tara and her niece stranded in a snowstorm. All because of the nagging fear that he was doomed to fail these two precious people.

"I haven't told you the important part, Gabe." Tara's fingers closed around his forearm. "Law enforcement knows but cannot prove in a court of law that Frazier launders money for multiple West Coast crime syndicates. Like a one-man criminal clearing house. His personal presence is a bit of a joke, but he's vital to a lot of ruthless people."

He jerked like he'd been punched. "They're going to take his happiness seriously, then." The weight returned and redoubled in his gut.

"If he whines to them, I have no idea what might come at us, where, or how soon."

Gabe's mouth went dry. While they'd successfully taken themselves off the radar of Sofie's vicious and dirty dad, unintended circumstances had potentially brought them to the attention of a whole bunch of bad folks who could be worse.

# EIGHT

Tara gnawed at her bottom lip, lost in thoughts that darted from one problem to the next, seeking solutions like Gabe's coonhound on a twisted trail. Sofie had been lulled back to sleep, as car rides tended to do for small children, which wasn't optimal in this circumstance. By the time they stopped this evening for the grown-ups to rest, the toddler might be wide-awake for half the night. But that was an issue for later. Right now, they must figure out how best to disappear so not even the pervasive tentacles of organized crime could feel them out.

"I keep thinking about your mention of trailering the Lancer. If we did that, the car would be out of sight."

Gabe's words drew Tara from her knotted thinking. "Where would we get a trailer?"

"Look on that map for the nearest large town or city where we could rent one."

"As well as something to pull it with."

"You know it."

"Helena isn't far from here."

Gabe pursed his lips. "Big city. Lots of eyes on us. Very much on the route we would be expected to take."

"There's Bozeman, but that's farther away and is also a major city on a freeway. Hmm. Now I miss having phone access to the internet. I could look up the nearest rental places. It's hard to say if any smaller out-of-the-way towns would have that sort of business."

She gazed around them. They had been driving through the rural countryside for a while. The view went on for miles, and homesteads were few and far between on rolling terrain. Occasionally, she'd noted items of machinery or vehicles with for-sale signs on them parked on the freeze-browned grass near driveways, but nothing that would serve their needs. What was she hoping? That a U-Haul or Ryder truck would be waiting for them on the side of the road?

"That'll do it." Gabe accompanied his words with a turn of the steering wheel onto a gravel driveway.

An aging crew-cab pickup sat on the berm. A rectangle of cardboard in the front window listed a price for the white truck, sporting rumples and dings, as well as a few bubbled-paint age spots.

Tara shot Gabe a questioning look. "What about your car?"

"I'm hoping the truck's owner will store it in his barn for a fee. I can come back whenever this is over and get it."

"But what about your memorial trip to Provo?"

He frowned at her and shook his head. "No car show is more important than you and Sofie's safety...and mine too."

"No, but I just meant—"

"I know, and I appreciate that you care about my life and the plans I had. You're a good person, and you don't deserve what's happening."

"Neither do you."

"Who's to say?"

That darkness Tara had glimpsed in him from time to time flitted across his face, then disappeared, sucked into the black hole where he kept some private devastation.

The Lancer rolled to a stop in front of a single-story ranch-style home with a wide porch along the front. The large farm site also hosted a sizeable machine shed, a big red barn in need of paint and a clapboard outbuilding that didn't look like it had ever been painted. A couple of horses moved around in a corral attached to the barn, and in the distance, a small herd of cows grazed in a large pasture. Either the people who owned the place were off working somewhere or they were in the house.

With the cessation of the car's movement, Sofie woke up and whimpered. Tara turned toward her as Gabe got out of the vehicle, admitting a waft of chilly air flavored with odors of hay and manure.

Gabe stuck his head back inside the car. "I'll go to the door. See if anyone's home."

"I'll give Sofie a snack and see if she'll settle again. I'm sure she's fed up with being strapped into her car seat."

He closed the door and headed for the two steps leading onto the porch while Tara turned her attention to finding some nibbles for the fussing toddler. Macky had roused and was sitting alertly to one side of Sofie's car seat, attentive eyes following his master's progress toward the house.

Tara quickly found out she'd been correct in her assessment of Sofie's mood. The toddler wanted to be out of the car seat, and she was being vocal about her desire. She didn't want a snack. She just wanted freedom. Now. Tara glanced toward the porch and discovered Gabe was speaking to someone who had come to the door. She couldn't see the person. The shadows were too thick under the porch roof. But maybe the inhabitant would be kind enough to allow her to bring Sofie inside to change her diaper.

Sighing, Tara got out of the car, opened the rear door and unbuckled her niece. Mentally, she prepared a winsome speech to the homeowner who may be reluctant to invite a stranger in, even with an adorable toddler in tow. Preparing herself to grovel, even if only a little bit, Tara turned toward the house with Sofie in her arms and her mouth open to speak.

The words died on her tongue as she spotted a smiling middle-aged woman in jeans and a sweatshirt standing on the edge of the porch and motioning her to come inside. Answering the smile, Tara gave the woman a small wave, grabbed her niece's diaper bag and wasted no time accepting the invitation. Their hostess's welcoming expression didn't dim at all as Macky followed along on Tara's heels.

"Come on in out of the cold." Still beaming, the woman, whose short curly hair was more salt than pepper, closed the door after the little troupe.

Gabe was already standing in the small tile-floored foyer that opened into a living area populated with well-worn but comfortable furniture, and farther back was an open-plan kitchen decorated in cozy country style. Warmth and the scent of cinnamon and baking apples enfolded Tara.

"Thank you." She nodded toward their hostess. "I'm Tara, this is Sofie." She bounced the little girl in her arms. Thankfully, the toddler had stopped fussing and was looking around with interest.

"And that's Macky." Gabe spoke up, gesturing toward his dog. "And I already introduced myself, Mrs. Burns."

The woman lifted a hand. "Shelly, please. Let's relax in the living room and talk." She led the way by going to an easy chair and perching on its edge.

Gabe followed and sat on one end of the sofa. Tara followed and sank onto the sofa's other end while removing Sofie's warm outerwear. The little girl wriggled to be let down, but Tara hung on to her.

"It's all right. Let her be." Shelly laughed and pulled a basket forward from beside her chair. Toys filled the basket, and Sofie squealed. "Our daughter has two, one a little older than yours and one a little younger. I keep these things for when they come to visit."

"If you're sure it won't be any trouble."

"Probably be more fuss to keep the child away from the toys."

Gabe's mellow laugh rumbled. "Literally."

"Well, okay. Here goes." Grinning, Tara released Sofie, who toddled eagerly toward the playthings, Macky at her heels.

"Mrs.—er, Shelly, we *are* interested in the truck you have for sale, but we also need to ask a favor. We'll pay, but—"

The hostess lifted a forestalling hand. "Let's wait a few minutes for my husband, Pete, to get here before we talk business. I called him when I saw you drive up."

"That was prudent." Tara gave the woman an approving look. "You never know these days."

The woman chuckled. "At first, caution was my thought, but a couple tootling around the back roads of Montana in a 1950s car with a baby and a dog in the back seat are unlikely to be Bonny and Clyde wannabes."

Tara bit her lip and looked toward Gabe, who had dropped his gaze toward his shoes. What should they tell this woman and her husband when he showed up? No, they weren't desperate criminals, but they *were* desperate. And the people after them made the notorious gangster couple look like Sunday School teachers.

How willing would the Burns be to help them if they knew the risks? Sure, the likelihood of their enemies tracing their route to this location was minimal. But not nonexistent. Gabe and she could withhold full disclosure to get what they wanted with few questions, but that felt dishonest, even wicked, to involve other people unwittingly in their mess.

The atmosphere seemed to gather extra weight, as if gravity had suddenly grown stronger. The next few minutes would either see them on their way in new wheels—or rather shabby, nondescript wheels—the shining classic car hidden away—or they would be on their way. Period. Out into the wild in a vehicle that could be drawing venomous eyes even as they sat here in this cozy cinnamon-scented living room. More and more, Tara was realizing that safety was an illusion.

Standing outside in the chilly air, Gabe kept his hands in his jacket pockets and a rein on his hopes as the grizzled rancher cupped his chin in his palm and rubbed the sides of his jaw with his thumb and fingers. The man walked around the Lancer, studying the vehicle closely.

"Mighty fine old Dodge, but nope. I don't want to store a car here that gangsters are hunting for."

Gabe's heart sank, but he couldn't blame Pete Burns for the decision. He huffed out a long breath. There was no point in buying the old pickup truck if they couldn't get the classic car out of sight at the same time.

Pete had arrived home from errands in town about half an hour ago and turned out to be just as friendly as his wife. Neither Pete nor Shelly had wanted to hear a word about business until they'd all enjoyed some of Shelly's apple crisp, which was delicious. Then, finally, they'd gotten down to negotiations while Sofie played happily with the Burns' grandkids' toys, oblivious to the serious situation.

Gabe had been honest about their reason for wanting

alternate transportation and the need to get the Lancer out of sight, but he'd omitted any mention of the situation involving Sofie and her dangerous father, earning a nod of approval from Tara. The former was relevant to their potential transaction with the ranchers, but the latter was not. However, now that Pete had opted out of storing the Lancer, the whole issue was moot, and Gabe should round up his little troupe so they could get on the road, searching for the next opportunity.

"But I got another idea." The rancher turned and fixed Gabe with what he could only describe as a sly smirk. "Follow me." Waving at Gabe to follow him, the man headed off toward the machine shed in his rolling bow-legged gait.

Pursing his lips, Gabe trailed after the spry man in his early sixties. What alternative could the rancher have in mind? They entered the cavernous metal building through a side door designed for humans rather than pulling aside the massive double doors on rollers at the front. Odors of diesel fuel, motor oil, grease and cold cement greeted them. Pete flipped a switch, and banks of fluorescent lights beamed down from the rafters, illuminating the ample space occupied by tractors and implements, like a rake and a baler, as well as a stock trailer with vents for hauling horses, cows or other farm animals.

Pete led the way down the side of the building, past shelves full of parts and tools, until they reached the far corner. The rancher waved a hand at a fully enclosed trailer. The white body with black trim was dulled by dust but otherwise appeared sturdy. This sort of wheeled conveyance was only suitable for transporting inanimate objects, such as small farm implements or a moderate-sized vehicle. Perfect for hauling a 1959 Dodge Custom Royal Lancer Super D-500 sedan. Neat, sweet and out of sight.

"Wow." Gabe walked down the side of the trailer, checking out the wheels, which looked good. "Just wow."

He turned and met Pete's steady gaze, and words died on his tongue. He'd expected a wide smile, as the man enjoyed the surprise he'd sprung, but instead the rancher's demeanor conveyed a deep and abiding grief.

"I'm sorry." Gabe uttered the words without knowing why.

"It's okay." Pete's gaze dropped, and he scuffed a boot toe against a crack in the cement beneath his feet. "Our younger son, Ronnie's hobby was racing stock cars at all the local tracks around the state and down into Wyoming, too. He had a need for speed." The man patted the side of the trailer, producing a hollow rattle. "But then…well, he passed." The rancher's eyes turned glassy, and he sniffed, but a tear never fell.

"Accident on the track?"

"Nope." Pete shook his head. "Leukemia. Came on like a freight train. He was gone in a few months. Not sure why Shelly and I have hung on to this trailer. Ronnie's best friend bought the stock car from us, and we figured our son would want it for him. However, for some reason, we just parked this trailer and tried to forget its existence. Now, the thing might do someone some good. Ronnie would like that, too. You interested?"

"Can the pickup truck at the end of your drive pull it?"

"Yup. That old Ram 1500 is a workhorse. Terrible gas mileage, but it'll get the job done."

"Then you've got a deal." Gabe held out his hand toward Pete, and the rancher's calloused paw responded with a firm clasp.

Within an hour after paying the Burns electronically through a finance app on their home computer and helping Pete move his machinery out of the way so the trailer could be hooked up to the pickup, Gabe and the rancher maneuvered the Lancer into the sturdy trailer and secured it with ratchet straps and wheel chocks. Meanwhile, Tara transferred their goods, including Sofie's car seat, from the Lancer into the Ram. Gabe noted that the crew-type cab positioned the baby seat closer to the front seat than a car or a club cab would have, which might prove convenient for Tara to pass things like snacks back to Sofie or otherwise keep the child happy while they put serious distance beneath the tires today. Sure, anyone spotting their rig would assume the trailer was hauling *something*, but no one could see inside to know for sure. To Gabe's way of thinking, the other vital factor in getting clean away was vacating the area where the classic car had been seen by greedy eyes.

Gabe exchanged a final handshake with Pete and accepted a hug from Shelly. The ranching couple gave Tara the same treatment, and Shelly tickled a happily gabbling Sofie under the chin. Then Tara installed her niece in the car seat, and Gabe ushered his dog into the rear of the pickup cabin on the driver's side. Then he took his place behind the wheel. The cab smelled of pine from a deodorizer that hung from a radio knob, with an underlying hint of fresh-mown hay, befitting a ranch work truck.

Tara hopped in and buckled up, offering Gabe a glance and a small smile. He returned the smile and headed the truck and trailer rig down the driveway toward the paved county road. No sooner had the wheels hit the tarmac than a giggle burst from Tara's lips.

"What?" Gabe's brows drew together.

"That was *amazing*! God led us here. Don't you see?"

A laugh bubbled up from Gabe's chest. "I think you're

right. There's no way this specialized provision popped up out of nowhere for no reason."

They looked at each other and burst out laughing again. An almost giddy sound. Then, suddenly, Tara's hilarity morphed into weeping. Not gentle tears, but deep gut-wrenching sobs. Immediately, Sofie joined the chorus with alarmed baby wails. Macky whined and then let out the distinctive redbone coonhound howl. Heart in his throat, Gabe began slowing the rig, intending to pull over onto the narrow gravel verge.

Tara rolled her hands, indicating he should continue driving. She hiccupped and pressed her forearms against her middle. The sobs subsided into simple deep breathing. In response, the baby and the dog also began to quiet.

"I'm…sorry." Her words came out with a little hitch between them. "It's been so long since I sensed God's care for me that seeing evidence of His intervention overwhelmed me." She turned and reached back toward Sofie. Gabe assumed she was patting her niece. "I'm okay, sweetheart." The child gurgled, and the crying turned into a small giggle. "That's right, honey. The doggy loves you."

Tara faced forward once more and heaved out a sigh. "Macky is licking away her tears, and I think his tongue tickles her." Her gaze met Gabe's, but she quickly looked away. "I'm okay," she repeated.

"Are you really?" Gabe voiced the question in a low tone.

She shook her head. "But I *will* be. I have to be. For Sofie."

Gabe's respect for Tara took a fresh spike. The months of helping her sister deal with a fugitive ex and a new baby, then stepping in on her sister's murder and stopping the kidnapping of Sofie must have been beyond horrible. Now, with no time to process her own grief, much less help a confused and bereft child deal with her emotions, as the sole carer for her niece, Tara found herself under constant threat from a ruthless criminal and his hirelings. The stress had to be off the charts. She was entitled to blow off a little steam with an emotional outburst.

"Relax." He reached out and gave her hand a squeeze, then returned his grip to the steering wheel. "Take a nap if you want. I plan to get us into Wyoming by suppertime. Then I'd like to be halfway through that state before we stop for the night."

Tara nodded, settled her head against the rest and closed her eyes.

Silence blanketed the truck cab. Miles passed smoothly beneath the wheels. Rancher Pete had been right. The Ram was a workhorse, displaying no trouble pulling the load. As Gabe had told Tara, he stuck to back roads, which resulted in a lot of meandering and slowing down as he passed through small towns, some so tiny that their populations did not exceed three digits. If Frazier had people looking for them, they would deserve a medal and a bonus for conquering the needle-in-a-haystack challenge. How long their incognito could last, he had no way of predicting, but he'd take full advantage of traveling free and clear of any threats.

True to Gabe's plan, they ate supper shortly after crossing into Wyoming. They even visited a big-box store for a few changes of clothes, hygiene supplies and other necessary items for Sofie. Then they drove on. When darkness fell and Sofie started to get cranky, they stopped for the night at a mom-and-pop motel in a small town smack in the middle of the state where the Bighorn Mountains loomed on one side and rolling ranchland sprawled on the other. A twenty-four-hour diner across the street from the motel offered them an opportunity for a bedtime snack and hydration. Then the motel's owners gratefully accepted cash for one night, with no credit card required.

They settled into the clean but plain two-bed unit on the ground floor and took turns in the bathroom. The toddler fell asleep almost immediately after being cleaned up and placed in a one-piece sleeper. As a sleepy silence settled over the room, Gabe parted the curtain an inch and studied the parking lot. Ambient light from the diner opposite the motel splashed partially across the road, but didn't lap up against the motel's parking lot, where darkness and silence ruled. Headlights passed on the road, but only a few and far between. He felt fairly confident about their safety, but not so cocky that he turned down Tara's idea that she should keep watch for the first half of the night. Gabe was bushed. He'd been driving all day, and she'd had a nap. He did, however, remain dressed in jeans and a T-shirt, rather than sleepwear, in case quick action became necessary.

"Wake me up in a few hours, and I'll spell you." Gabe reached down and patted his dog's head. "Macky's nose and ears will be hard to sneak up on, too. If he gets antsy, pay attention."

Then he placed his loaded gun, safety on, under his pillow and settled into the bed across the room from Tara and Sofie's. Dreamless sleep swallowed him whole until a harsh canine growl and a muted human cry pierced the oblivion.

"Gabe! Wake up! They've found us!"

# NINE

Tara's eyes widened as Gabe went from sound asleep to alert in a split second. She backed away as he slid smoothly from under the covers and rose, gun in hand. Clearly, his Special Forces training hadn't left him. That stone-cold light gleamed in his eyes, chilling yet grounding her in a sense of security.

She mentally shook herself. There was no safety while hunters prowled for them.

Gabe shushed his dog with a wordless command motion. Macky's growl subsided, though his sleek body remained taut and at attention.

Gabe's gaze met hers. "Sit rep." His words were soft but urgent.

*Sit rep? Oh, situation report.*

"A dark sedan pulled into the parking lot a few minutes ago, but they didn't park in a guest spot, and the engine didn't shut off. Whoever was in it sat there for a while, and I wasn't sure if they were innocent travelers deciding whether to check in. But then the driver and a passenger got out. I don't think anyone else is in the vehicle, but I believe they are holding guns. They're keeping the weapons down and at their sides, more or less out of sight. They seem to be slinking around, peering into the cars in the parking lot."

Gabe nodded. "Looking for a child seat to suggest we are here and what we are driving." He paced past her on soundless bare feet, tugged the curtain aside a slight margin. "They're still looking, and I think you're right. They're holding weapons. Good thing we parked behind the motel. They won't find our rig right away." He turned and moved toward the bathroom. "I'm going to go out the bathroom window and retrieve the car seat. Wait at the window and take it from me. I don't want them identifying our transportation by its presence if they manage to sneak past me for a look around the back lot."

"Sneak past you?" Tara followed in his wake. "What are you going to do?"

"Go hunting." He glanced over his shoulder at her, wearing a shark smile.

Tara shivered, but her heart lightened. She would *not* want to be those guys out there. Funny how Gabe's dangerous persona conveyed hope.

In less than a minute, Tara laid the car seat on the bathroom floor while Gabe disappeared into the moonlight, a shadow within a shadow. She moved into the main room and retrieved her pistol from the nightstand drawer even as she checked on Sofie. The little girl sprawled like a contented starfish under the covers, sound asleep. Her beloved bear had somehow gotten flung to the foot of the bed.

Tara picked up the stuffed animal and began kneading it like a stress toy in one hand while the other clutched her gun. *Please, God, let me not have to use a firearm near my niece. She's been exposed to too much gunfire in a couple of short days.* Using the barrel of the pistol, she parted the curtain enough to see out.

One suspicious character was busy checking out the last of the vehicles in the front lot, but the other armed creeper had disappeared. Had the guy gone inside to question the desk attendant? If so, he probably wouldn't hear about a woman with a toddler in tow occupying one of the rooms. Gabe had checked them into the motel while Tara stayed in the truck with Sofie. According to him, the incurious attendant hadn't even asked who else was going to occupy the two-bed motel room he'd paid for. Hopefully, she and Sofie hadn't been spotted when they got out of the truck and went in, but there was no way to know for sure. Tara's stomach clenched.

The guy checking the vehicles went around the far side of the hotel toward the back lot, and she lost sight of him. Tara backed away from the window. She had to trust Gabe to do what was necessary out there, while she packed up their belongings in preparation for a clean getaway. Hopefully.

How had these people found them? Were they mob heavies or mercs sent by Zander? Tara leaned toward the latter.

Gritting her teeth against a frustrated outburst, Tara gave the bear's belly a convulsive squeeze. Something hard deep inside the stuffing drew her attention. Her mouth went dry.

On swift silent feet, she entered the bathroom, set her gun on the vanity and began to examine the bear, aided by the moon and starlight glowing faintly through the window. She'd never looked at the object closely before, mostly because she associated the toy with Zander's toxic pseudo-love. If Sofie weren't so attached to the stuffed animal, she would have thrown the bear in the trash long ago.

*There!* A few inches along one side seam showed signs of having been slit open and then sewn shut less professionally than the rest of the body. Tara quickly retrieved the miniature scissors from the travel sewing kit in Sofie's bag. With shaking hands, she reopened the seam, then fished inside the fluff until her fingers closed around a small round object. She pulled the offensive item out and glared at the hard case resting in the palm of her hand.

A soft rap sounded on the door, and tiny ant-feet skittered up Tara's spine. She dropped the bear on the floor, stuck the device in her jeans pocket and picked up her gun. Silently, she moved into the main room and stood to the side of the door, gun at the ready.

"It's me. Open up."

Gabe. Tension leached from Tara's shoulders, and she lowered the pistol. She quickly undid the chain, unlocked the door and opened it just far enough for him to sidle through the gap, drawing with him a waft of chilly air. Tara shivered, but not only from the cold. That small hard object she'd just found inside Teddy was a GPS device—they were being tracked. No wonder they could never seem to elude Zander's mercs for long.

"We need to go before those two scouts wake up, or any reinforcements arrive for them."

"Scouts? Wake up?"

Gabe shrugged. "I'll explain on the road."

"We need to deal with this." Tara pulled the device out of her pocket and thrust it toward him.

He took the object from her with a frown. "Where was this?"

"Teddy. How is it possible for the thing to still work? Zander gave the bear to Sofie before she was born. Then he disappeared right afterward."

"Another conversation for the road. I've got an idea on how to use the tracker for misdirection." He turned and gripped the doorknob. "Get everything together and hand our belongings to me through the bathroom window. We'll exit the room that way also." Then he was gone like a puff of smoke.

Questions buzzing around her brain, Tara got busy gathering up their things. She carried everything into the bathroom and found Gabe approaching the window. He'd started the truck. The diesel engine growled softly, and the exhaust pipes emitted a trail of white mimicked by Gabe's and her breath in the chilly air. She handed him the child seat first so he could reinstall it for Sofie's use. Within ten minutes, the truck was loaded.

"Send Macky through." Gabe reached through the window toward his dog, who stood nearby, tail wagging.

Tara knelt and pushed the hound's rear end while Gabe pulled. Macky flexed his hind legs and scrabbled against the wall, ejecting himself out the window all at once. Gabe staggered backward with a little chuckle and deposited his dog on the ground. The faithful redbone followed his master toward the truck while Tara turned away, steeling herself to disturb Sofie's sleep to bundle her up and transport her. The little girl despised having her slumber interrupted and was likely to register her displeasure. Hopefully not so loudly that they awakened anyone in adjoining rooms.

The bundling operation went more smoothly than Tara had dared to imagine, especially when she begrudgingly returned the debugged traitor bear to the little girl's waiting arms. However, Sofie clearly didn't care about the idea of getting back in her car seat and put up a fuss until Macky licked her cheek and rested his head on her lap. Despite the minor struggle, within five minutes, they were leaving the motel and the little town in the rearview.

Tara settled herself into a more comfortable position and unzipped her jacket now that the vehicle was warming up nicely. "Spill, buster. What did you do with the two creepers and the tracking device?"

Gabe's grin gleamed in the darkness. "The creepers, as you so appropriately put it, are taking naps in their car courtesy of fists to glass jaws. I parked the vehicle properly with them inside, but left the engine running and the heat on, so they won't get hypothermic before they wake up and help each other work loose from the duct tape around their hands and feet."

"Duct tape?"

"Yep. They conveniently had a roll in their glove compartment. I used it and then I kept it. Most versatile tool on the planet. I also relieved them of their cell phones and destroyed them."

"And the tracker?"

"A pair of good ol' boys were slurping coffee and inhaling biscuits and gravy in the diner across the street. I tossed that vicious little disc into the bed of their late-model Chevy club cab. They should be well on their way to wherever they're going by the time Creep 1 and Creep 2 get loose with their wits about them. When they catch up to the device, they'll find a pair of rough-around-the-edges cowboys, but not an attractive US deputy marshal and her cute niece. I'd pay to be a fly on the wall and witness the mercs' reactions."

*Attractive?* Tara's cheeks warmed at the slip of the tongue, but she refrained from calling him out on it. Especially when such a conversation might lead to a verbal admission that she returned the sentiment.

She shook her head. "I still don't understand how the device can be transmitting after all this time."

"You can get high-end trackers that remain dormant until remotely activated, and then they only transmit a ping at a prescribed interval, stretching the battery life significantly. At some point, Zander activated the tracker. Probably when you got custody."

Tara's blood chilled. All these months, Linnea and then Tara placated Sofie with that bear, having no idea the thing could be as deadly as a ticking bomb, leading killers to them wherever they went. Now, the tracker was gone. Out of their lives. Would Zander also be out of their lives?

Tara knew better. A frustrated Zander could act out in ways none of them could begin to conceive. No, the danger continued with no end in sight.

The seemingly endless winding road flowed beneath their tires, holding Gabe's attention on the white lines spooling past in the darkness. However, he remained acutely conscious of the woman next to him. Tara had gone silent. Probably gnawing her lower lip and staring sightlessly into the night. He'd come to recognize the posture as her post-trauma processing behavior.

The dash clock said 4:00 a.m., so he'd managed a few hours of shuteye before she'd awakened him about the arrival of those dangerous men. Still, fatigue sat hard in his core without rendering him sleepy. He'd felt this way many times in his career as a PJ. Yet, the cost of failure had never weighed more heavily. Not even during his last mission, which went tragically sideways in an astonishing instant. Gabe shifted in his seat as his insides wrung painfully.

"Are you all right?"

Tara's soft-voiced question feathered warmth into his chilled heart.

"Ye—" He started to dissemble, then thought better of the pretense. "Not really."

"I've noticed that when we're under immediate threat,

you go into machine mode, and nothing rattles you. But when we're in the between times, something about your role in protecting us has you as uncomfortable as a cat in a room full of rocking chairs."

"Uncomfortable? Nope. Terrified, yes."

"Is that emotional state normal for a trained PJ?"

"I'm not..." He swallowed convulsively against a dry throat. "There's a reason why I'm not a PJ anymore."

Tara's body angled toward him. "You can talk about it. Or not, if you don't want to. Either way, I trust you."

Her words speared through Gabe's core, and a pained bark wrung from his lips. "You trust me? What if I don't trust myself? Not completely. Not anymore."

"You lost someone."

"Not some*one*." Gabe shook his head like a dog shedding water. "Everyone."

An indrawn breath hissed sharply. "I'm... I'm so sorry. Accident?"

"No accidents during combat when someone's really trying to kill you, and it's the para team's job to either stop them or get our people out of harm's way. Unforeseen circumstances. Yup. Bad intel. Maybe. Equipment failure. Sometimes."

"Which was it for you?"

"All of the above."

"Sounds like a perfect storm. I'm amazed you survived."

"But I was the only one. My teammates. Closer than family. And a whole squad of elite ground troops all gone in a blaze of bullets and bombs courtesy of militants who weren't supposed to be there. My PJ team went in to rescue survivors from a helicopter that went down because its missile avoidance countermeasures failed to deploy. After our aircraft destroyed the enemy's missile nest, we jumped to the location of the crash, patched up the wounded and then began to move everyone to a new LZ."

"LZ?"

"Landing zone. The supposedly safe designated pickup spot for my team and the evacuees."

"Supposedly safe?"

"Our intel hadn't caught up to the fact that war had suddenly broken out between enemy tribes in the area. We wound up crushed between the warring factions who suddenly had a common foe—us."

"I can hardly imagine." She let out a soft whimper. "Must have been beyond intense."

"Yup. We fought like our lives depended on it—because they did. But there were too many of them and insufficient cover. We were going down like flies. Then one of the opposition forces lobbed a grenade. I saw it coming and fell on top of the wounded soldier I had been helping to navigate toward the LZ. The world went black. I woke up in the hospital, peppered with shrapnel holes and a few bad burns. Turns out the Air Force sent out a second PJ team to pull us out of there, but all they found was a massacre. The guy I had tried to shield from the grenade had bled out beneath me while I was bleeding on him." Gabe released a long shuddering sigh. "Spent the rest of my tour recovering on base Stateside. I didn't re-up. The Air Force waved goodbye to me with a Bronze Star and a Purple Heart, but they couldn't give me what I really wanted."

Tara's hand closed around one of his, and she wrapped it close against her body. "Your team."

"Yes, and the soldiers we were sent to save."

In that moment, the warmth of her hand and the solemn silence of her mourning alongside him soothed the hurt more profoundly than the hours of counseling therapy he'd endured before his discharge.

Gabe took a long deep breath and then another. "Thank you."

"For what?"

"Just for listening and not judging."

"Why would I judge what was beyond your control? You give everything to those you serve. I know firsthand, and I'm gratefully amazed by your dedication to virtual strangers like Sofie and me. Whatever happened out there on that battlefield, I have no doubt you gave your all. In a personal sense, that's the opposite of failure, regardless of the outcome in a mission sense. I do see, though, how your heart would insist that you'd failed because the loss was so profound, but your heart is lying to your head. Only you can call the heart a deceiver and allow yourself to heal from what happened without false blame getting in the way."

Gabe let out a wounded snicker. "Easier said than done."

"Don't I know it." Tara released his hand and rubbed her palms across her face. "Many times, my thoughts torment me with what-ifs. Especially, what if I had arrived a few minutes sooner at my sister's house that day? Could I have saved her from the assassin's knife? But that didn't happen, and no amount of coulda-shoulda-woulda can change reality. I can only go forward, doing everything in my power to protect my niece. If I fail to keep her safe, I doubt I'll survive. Or even want to."

"We're on the same page there. Only for me, it's protecting *both* of you." He grimaced. "I tried hard not to let it happen, but you two have gotten under my skin. When I'm out there in the park as a ranger performing search and rescue duties, the process seems like a job—one I'm trained to do well, but it's not personal. For some reason, it is this time. I need to ensure your and Sofie's safety or die trying."

She huffed. "Let's work on neither of us dying."

"Agreed."

"For right now, maybe we should think about finding someplace to eat breakfast. My empty tummy is throwing a tantrum."

They chuckled simultaneously, and the weight of grief in the cab dissipated. Was he mistaken, or had they reached a fresh level of comfort and trust in one another's presence? If so, what did that mean? Something more permanent that came after this constant cycle of running skirmishes?

If there *was* an after.

Gabe yanked his wayward thoughts away from vaguely formed hopes and dreams. *Stick with the present, buddy. Safer for you and for them. And safer for your heart.*

False dawn had begun to loosen the grip of night on the sprawling landscape of rolling hills gashed with steep arroyos. They would hit Casper, Wyoming, before long. A good stopping place for breakfast.

"If we can find one of those fast-food restaurants featuring a play area for small children, that would be best." Tara's head turned toward the rear compartment and her niece, who was beginning to make mewling noises. "She needs to run around and stretch her legs a bit before we head onward."

Gabe grunted an acknowledgment. "Macky could use a walk around the block, too, for that matter."

Within half an hour, they'd reached the outskirts of Casper and located an eating spot, just in time to forestall a full-blown wail from the toddler. Tara headed inside to take Sofie to the ladies' room to be cleaned up before they ordered breakfast. Gabe put Macky on his lead and went for that turn around the block in the brisk early morning air. He took the opportunity to conduct some reconnaissance and was pleased to note that there was no sign they were being followed or observed. Soon, he left Macky in the truck with some fresh kibble in a dog dish they'd bought at the big-box store the day before, as well as a small bowl of fresh water poured from one of a 12-pack of bottles they'd likewise purchased at the store yesterday.

The fast-food restaurant embraced him with warmth, the hum of conversation, and the mouthwatering scent of sausages and eggs. He spied Tara at a corner booth, watching her niece play in a pool of plastic balls. She noticed him and waved, then lifted three fingers and pointed to herself. Gabe's glance at the menu board showed that selection to be the bacon, egg and cheese biscuit meal. Then she blew on the tips of her fingers like she was cooling them down, followed by pointing toward Sofie. Hotcakes for the toddler. *Gotcha.* Grinning, Gabe made the okay sign with his fingers and got into line to order. The full breakfast with hotcakes was calling his name.

Soon, they were enjoying warm and filling food. Just like a real family. Gabe shoved that sneaky, dangerous notion away from him, but still it lurked in the wings, as they shared bits of eggs and sausage from their meals with Sofie, who wolfed everything down, including every bite of her hotcakes. The little girl had been hun-n-n-gry.

Then she was ready to play again, and Tara didn't seem eager to leave. Gabe shrugged and leaned back in the booth. Was it too much to ask for a brief respite to enjoy their coffee? Despite the regular glances out the window to remain aware of their surroundings, Gabe had no problem indulging the small comfort. Soon, he was up and laughing with Sofie as he caught her again and again at the bottom of the small slide. Tara's smile and the light in her eyes as she watched them sent waves of warmth through Gabe's chest. For the first time in a long time, life seemed more to be savored than endured. But, at last, Sofie became tired and started rubbing her eyes.

Tara scooped her up. "I'll take her to the ladies' room again to freshen her up before we get on the road."

Gabe patted Sofie's round cheek and shared a smile with Tara. "You come on out when you're ready. I'll go start the truck and see if Macky needs to step out before we go."

"Sounds like a plan."

Humming The Platters' 1955 version of "Only You, and You Alone," Gabe strode across the asphalt toward the truck and trailer they had parked at the back of the parking lot, where there was plenty of room for the long rig. Macky's head showed above the rear of the driver's seat. He sat quietly, tongue lolling—a good sign that all remained well. Gabe let the dog out, took him to a bush-lined grassy verge between the restaurant and a gas station, then put the hound back in the vehicle.

He glanced toward the restaurant. No sign yet of Tara and Sofie. Mild unease wafted through him, but he shook it off. She was preparing both herself and a toddler for another few hours on the road, so the process might take extra time. Turning away, Gabe checked the trailer hitch and found the connection as it should be. Then he went to the rear of the trailer and tugged the padlock securing the doors. Everything remained secure.

Suddenly, Macky let out a howl. Gabe went still, except for his gaze darting side to side. Movement from the bushes. He started to turn, but the distinctive cough of a suppressed gunshot, along with the spang of a bullet striking the asphalt near his feet, froze him in place.

"Don't turn around." A voice, rough like sandpaper, snarled the order. "Why don't you just go ahead and open that trailer while you're at it? Let's see what you got in there. If it's not what we want, then you might live to see another day. And if it *is* what we want, well, there's gotta be consequences for disrespectin' the wrong person."

# TEN

Tara stepped out of the restaurant, adjusting the strap of the diaper bag over her shoulder while clutching a wiggly toddler in the opposite arm. Sofie hadn't been cooperative in the ladies' room, so doing the necessary tasks had taken extra time, but now they were ready. Tara had even taken a few moments to press a cool paper towel against her puffy red eyes, courtesy of sleep deprivation. Once Sofie succumbed to a nap, Tara was going to take one too. She'd been awake for over twenty hours now, ever since her snooze yesterday afternoon.

As they crossed the parking lot, the chill air under overcast skies nipped her cheeks. Sofie's skin pinkened under the crisp breeze as well. As they drew near the pickup, Macky's frantic barking and the absence of Gabe in plain sight slowed Tara's steps. Heart hammering in her chest, she moved closer in cautious silence.

At last, voices reached her from the far end of the trailer. Tara couldn't see either of the speakers, but she identified Gabe's voice and one other. Someone who sounded like he gargled regularly with salt water. No mistaking the hostility in the tone, though she couldn't make out specific words of the conversation because of the background din.

The truck was running with its usual diesel rumble, and

Macky continued to bark and whine. Tara took advantage of the noise to mask the sounds of opening the rear door and slipping Sofie inside under the care of the redbone coonhound. The dog ceased barking and all but wrapped his sinuous body around the toddler, forestalling the irritated howl from Sofie that had seemed ready to break out, judging by the child's puckered face and stormy eyes. Her niece's expression smoothed, and the little girl flung her arms around the canine's neck.

*What a good dog.*

Tara unzipped the diaper bag and reached deep inside, beneath all the other contents, to locate her Glock pistol. What a messed-up world that a person would need to keep a firearm in an infant's carryall. But, at the same time, she was glad of the gun's presence. Taking up the stabilizing Weaver stance, she moved toward the rear of the rig, pistol leading the way.

Voice agitated and aggressive, the hostile guy snarled a threat at Gabe. Tara could wait no longer. She whipped around the corner, pointing the pistol toward the sound of the stranger's voice. A lean craggy-faced man halted in midsentence and gaped at her, even as he began to swivel his gun in her direction. Gabe moved with the suddenness and accuracy of a striking cobra. He swept the stranger's gun arm up and to the side with his left forearm, even while his right fist whooshed a powerful uppercut to the guy's pointy chin.

Tara's jaw dropped and her eyes widened at the meaty smack. The man's feet fully left the ground as he flew backward, splatted flat on his back, and lost his grip on his weapon, which skittered away. The guy lay still as a stone, eyes closed, out cold.

She lowered her pistol and blinked at Gabe. "I see what you mean about the fist to the glass jaw."

Gabe snorted, flexing his fingers. "My fist is getting

tired of the nonsense. Thanks for the distraction. I'm not sure if my maneuver would have worked without it."

Tara frowned at the stranger who was beginning to stir slightly. "What are we going to do with him?" She gazed around the area. Although people were out and about, no one seemed to have noticed what was happening in the corner of the parking lot, sheltered on two sides by five-foot-tall bushes and the bulky truck-and-trailer rig that blocked the view.

"To start with," Gabe nudged the downed aggressor with one toe, "put that duct tape to good use again. Watch him while I get it from the truck."

With a nod, Tara pointed her pistol muzzle toward the subdued hostile. Gabe quickly returned and began wrapping tape around the man's hands and feet, and then he slapped a strip across the guy's mouth as the man sprang awake and attempted to sit up.

"Stay still if you know what's good for you." Gabe nodded toward Tara, who held her pistol arms steady, and pressed the man back flat onto the asphalt.

Gabe stood and planted his hands on his hips, frowning at their prisoner. Tara took up a position beside him, her expression mirroring his, though she kept her gun trained on the guy, who glared at them as if wishing his storm-gray eyes were lasers.

"Okay, so we've got him subdued." Tara clucked her tongue. "I *can* arrest him as a United States deputy marshal, but the local police will have to take him into custody, and then they'll have jurisdiction. Do we want to go that route?"

"The local police will read him his rights and give him his phone call, and all of the formal processing steps, which means he'll have an opportunity to report to his bosses what we're driving."

"On the other hand, if we stash him in the bushes to let him work himself loose, he'll do the same thing, given time."

Gabe sighed. "I think—"

"Hold on a second." Tara squatted and studied their captive's face. Those razor-blade cheekbones. Those smoky eyes. And that left eyebrow with a scar bisecting it. "I know who this is. Carson 'Checkers' Rafferty." A grin grew on Tara's face even as Rafferty's eyes widened, and he began vigorously shaking his head. "Oh, yes, buster. There's a Most Wanted BOLO out on you as an escaped convict. In fact, you injured a transport guard badly when you escaped during a prison transfer last year. The US Marshals Service will gladly take jurisdiction and sweep you into custody—no phone call, no lawyer consultation, no court date—just a return to prison. Solitary, I'm guessing, for a good, long time while they sort out the new charges to be brought against you in addition to your already issued life sentence. Sounds like fun, huh?" She patted the man's cold cheek. "And what do you know? There's a US Marshals Field Office right here in Casper."

Tara swiveled her hips and looked up at a grinning Gabe. "Would you check on Sofie while I search this guy's pockets for his phone? I'll have to use it to call my boss in Great Falls, Montana, who will call the Casper, Wyoming, office to send someone over to collect this guy." She huffed. "The Service will be over the moon about this escapee's apprehension, but I'm not looking forward to the scolding I'm going to get from my supervisor for our disappearing act."

Gabe sent her a salute, turned on his heel and headed for the truck, which had gone peaceful and quiet, except for the purr of the engine. Macky must be taking good care of Sofie, and there had never been a risk that the toddler would climb into the front and put the truck in gear. She'd need to be big enough to plant her foot on the brake and strong enough to maneuver the stick. Neither operation was within the child's powers, much less doing those things simultaneously. Still, Tara was uneasy about the little girl being left without adult supervision for the past ten minutes.

Tara patted their prisoner down until she struck gold in the man's shirt pocket. She drew the phone out, woke the cell up and then forced Rafferty's thumbprint to open the device. Then she rose and towered over the prone convict, whose glare had gone decidedly sour as he contemplated all the consequences Tara had outlined to him.

Shaking her head, she began tapping in the number for the Great Falls field office. Once again, their attempt at covert escape from those who pursued them had been circumvented by the wrong eyes at the wrong place and time. Rafferty's appearance out of nowhere demonstrated that Frazier had indeed complained to his superiors, and now the widespread crews of multiple criminal organizations were on the lookout for them. Essentially, the underworld had put out a BOLO on Gabe's car, and by extension, their little band of misfits.

Yet, going back under the protection of the federal government seemed like a stopgap at best. Until Zander Wolf and Lix Frazier were incarcerated, none of them, she, Gabe or Sofie, could live freely and safely, no matter who attempted to look after them. Why did evil people's relentless ruthlessness seem to trump well-meaning efforts? The question seemed unanswerable.

Ah, well, the query was pointless at this moment. They needed to take the next step laid out before them. Tara tapped in the last number and placed the device against her ear. The screen's chill sent a shiver down her spine. The ringtone began to sound.

"Henderson here. I don't recognize the number. Is that you, Deputy Markson?" Her boss's tone contained eagerness, hope and yet anger, all in one conflicted stew.

Tara inhaled a deep breath and released the oxygen in a stream of pale condensation. *Here we go.*

Gabe sat quietly in a chair next to a side wall of the US Marshals field office bullpen, determined to remain largely unnoticed in the busy hub of activity. He'd already given a brief statement about the confrontation with the escaped convict in the restaurant parking lot, as well as the background information about Felix Frazier's interest in his vintage vehicle. Nobody seemed to require anything else from him for the moment, which was a relief. Rafferty had already been loaded into an armored van and was on his way back to prison, dripping with chains, and under the watchful eyes of three federal deputies armed to the eyeballs. That desperate character wasn't escaping custody again. Nor would he soon be communicating with anyone in the outside world.

Other deputies, most in uniforms identifying them as courtroom guards or prisoner escorts, came and went briskly from the spacious central hub of the Casper field office, populated by multiple workstations. Some of the deputies sat behind desks, focusing on their computers. Everyone seemed to have better things to do than study the stranger while US Deputy Marshal Tara Markson met with the deputy in charge of the Casper field office and her boss in Montana on a conference call in another room. What moments the deputies in the bullpen could spare were dominated by the undisputed star of the show: Little Miss Sofie.

The toddler moved from workstation to workstation, babbling happily but incomprehensibly to whomever she found at the desk. The occupant invariably turned their chair to smile and coo at the child. Then a desk drawer would open and out would come a treat—such as a snack cracker or small cookie—or even a toy, such as a squeeze ball—and Sofie would receive the offering as if it were her due. Gabe kept swallowing chuckles at the antics of the miniature adorable toll collector and her sidekick dog, who, as often as not, also received a treat.

Macky was well trained enough to cast a glance at his master before accepting each offering, and so far Gabe had nodded the go-ahead each time. Just for today. He wasn't eager to be the Scrooge of this lovefest. Thankfully, the coonhound possessed a cast-iron constitution, so he wasn't likely to develop stomach upset from the unusual consumption. If Sofie's eating became excessive or something toddler-inappropriate was offered, he'd call a halt, but so far, so good.

At last, Tara and the deputy in charge, a guy who'd introduced himself as Henry "call-me-Hank" Tickner, emerged from his office. She strode toward Gabe, and he rose, gut clenching. What had been decided behind those closed doors? Would he be bidding Tara and Sofie goodbye, perhaps never to see them again? The thought spiked nausea through him. But whatever was best for Tara and her niece is what they would do, regardless of the wrench to his emotions. How had he become so attached so quickly?

Tara stopped in front of him, her gaze shadowed. Gabe steeled himself against the hard news.

"The recommendation for now is that we go to a safe house."

"We?"

"You, me and Sofie."

"Me?"

Tara's brows arched like he'd gone slow on the uptake. Maybe he had.

"You're under threat from Lix Frazier's criminal associates. You need to lay low as much as Sofie and I do."

"Yes, but my situation is separate from yours."

She shook her head. "Somehow, everything has become intertwined. The Marshals Service has intelligence suggesting that Zander has put the word out about me and Sofie through the criminal organizations connected to Frazier, which ties our cases together."

"So, you're saying that the entire Northwestern underworld is after us?"

Tara's lips pursed, and she nodded. "Pretty much."

"Hanging out in a safe house isn't a lasting solution."

"Only until something more permanent can be arranged." The words appeared sour on her tongue because she grimaced.

"Like entering the witness protection program?" Gabe's gut went hollow. "Complete change of identity? I won't do it."

"I don't like the idea any better than you do." Her tone went sharp, and the buzz of conversation in the room halted. Tara ducked her head and cleared her throat. "I don't know what else to do."

The thin desperate whisper sliced through Gabe. He reached out to touch Tara's shoulder, but she turned away.

"Where's Sofie?" Her head swiveled this way and that. "Sofie, baby!"

"She's over here," a deputy at a desk near the back called out.

Tension visibly leached from Tara's body, and Gabe followed her across the room. There, tucked into a shadowed corner, Macky lay on his side with Sofie's head on his shoulder. The dog's four legs were curled protectively around the small body. Both appeared sound asleep. Then one of Macky's eyes opened a slit, and the coonhound offered a twitch of his tail in greeting. The eye slid closed once more.

"Awww." Tara's arms wrapped around one of Gabe's, and she rested her head against him. "So precious."

Gabe's heart swelled. Her trusting closeness felt right. So good. Perfect.

"We need to go to the safe house together." She lifted her head, and Gabe met her determined look. "How can we separate Sofie from her dog?"

"*Her* dog?" He smirked. "I think it would be cruel to separate *my* dog from his pet toddler."

Tara chuckled and smacked his arm with a gentle fist. "We should get going. The sooner the better."

"What about my truck and trailer rig? We sure don't want that parked in front of the safe house."

Behind them, a throat cleared, and Gabe turned to face Hank Tickner.

"We'd like to suggest getting the rig under cover in a rental storage unit for the time being."

"Sounds reasonable." Gabe nodded. "Since Rafferty never got the opportunity to let any of his confederates know he found us, no one trying to pick up our trail should know we're here in Casper."

Tickner nodded. "Might give us some breathing room to decide on the next course of action."

"Let's go, then."

Slightly over an hour later, Gabe's truck and trailer containing the vintage Dodge had been tucked out of sight in a pair of side-by-side rental units, and they were riding in the back of an unmarked SUV, pine-scented from an evergreen-shaped air freshener dangling from the rearview mirror. The SUV navigated a curvy little-traveled road leading up a mountainside. The vehicle was a bit crowded, with a pair of deputy marshals in the front seat, so Sofie, in her car seat, Tara, Gabe and Macky ended up stuffed into the rear. At least their bags, except for Sofie's diaper bag resting at Tara's feet, were in the cargo compartment behind them and not occupying their laps.

Gabe formed fists, then opened his hands and flexed his fingers. He should feel relieved to be under the Marshals Service's protection. Why didn't he?

Their escorts in the front seat seemed twitchy and kept exchanging glances. Slyness and conspiracy, or just operational nerves? Either way, their demeanor didn't inspire confidence.

He canted his head against the window glass and checked the rearview mirror. A breath hissed between his teeth. A black van was gaining on them with unhealthy speed on this winding road.

"We've got company." He made the announcement as much to inform Tara as to alert the deputy marshals.

"No worries." The deputy in the passenger seat cranked his head around and offered a toothy grin. "Probably just the people-mover van from the resort at the top of the mountain."

Why did the explanation seem glib rather than reassuring? Gabe clenched his jaw.

"Hey, Jimmy." The deputy poked the driver with a stiff finger. "Why don't we stop at the next overlook and let the van go past us?"

"Sounds like a good idea to me, Brad." The driver cast a glance toward the back seat. "I don't like another vehicle on our tail any more than Gabriel there."

What was with the white toothy grins on their escorts' faces? The two deputies couldn't be more different in appearance—one tall, one short, one lean, one beefy, one bald, one buzz-cut. And yet the Cheshire cat smiles matched each other in creepy wattage.

Even Tara saw the danger signals, if her narrow-eyed, scowling glance toward Gabe signaled concern. Gabe met her look and made a decision. That was it. He wasn't going to sit here unarmed and vulnerable like a penned sheep.

In one smooth movement, he unbuckled his seat belt, lunged upward and around, reaching for his bag in the cargo compartment. He should never have let them load him into this vehicle without his pistol under his belt. But he'd worried the Marshals Service would confiscate the weapon if he tried to bring it out. That concern was moot now.

One hand closed around the cloth of his duffel, and the other began to work the zipper. Two seconds, tops, had passed, and then Tara let out a small shriek, echoed by Sofie's startled cry and Macky's sharp bark. Something like a hard metal rod rammed into Gabe's back forcefully enough to bruise a kidney. A gun barrel? The answer seemed self-evident as pain speared through him, and a hissing grunt escaped his lips.

"Slow your roll there, buddy." Brad's tone landed somewhere between a purr and a snarl. "Let's not make this exchange more complicated than it needs to be."

White heat exploded in Gabe's middle. They'd been betrayed by the very people who should have been the most trustworthy.

# ELEVEN

A red mist settled across Tara's vision, and she lunged without a second thought. Grabbing the deputy's gun hand, she thrust one finger between the trigger and the guard, preventing him from discharging the weapon. With all her strength, she swept the man's arm upward. No way would she allow some lowlife to wave a gun in Sofie's general direction. Even though the pistol was aimed at Gabe, a bullet could easily go astray. Not that she wanted Gabe to get shot, either, but her niece was her priority.

Even as Tara struggled against her traitorous colleague to keep the pistol pointed skyward, Gabe inserted himself smoothly into the melee. He grabbed the gunman's wrist in both hands, wrenched the bones in a direction they weren't intended to move, and then caught the pistol that fell involuntarily from Brad's fingers. Tara withdrew her hand, and before she could catch her breath, Gabe slammed the gun butt against their attacker's skull. Brad, who had undone his seat belt and turned rearward to reach into the back seat and assault Gabe, now slumped awkwardly in the front bucket seat, facing the wrong direction with legs crumpled beneath him, disoriented and moaning.

Through the adrenaline roar in her ears, Tara could

barely discern the driver's impotent shouting that abruptly ceased when Gabe aimed the captured pistol at his head.

"Be quiet and drive." Gabe's tone emerged as a feral growl. "Do not stop until I tell you to do so."

The swerving that had begun during the brief struggle straightened out. Tara hauled in a long shaky breath, her mouth acrid with adrenaline's aftertaste. She'd been so focused on disarming the gunman she hadn't noticed how near the edge of the road their vehicle had strayed. The guardrails along this steep mountain grade may not have been enough to prevent their vehicle from plunging over a cliff.

"Where is our tail?"

Gabe's question settled Tara's spinning head. She looked behind them.

"Still there but falling back."

"They're likely wondering what's happening in here. I don't count on them going away, though."

"Me, either." Tara glared at the back of the bald driver's head. "What were you thinking? Betraying a child to a monster."

"Hey, a kid belongs with her dad." He shrugged. "I have no problem with that. And it was life-changing money. You know, the kind that gets you your own private island where you live like a king forever." The guy had begun to babble, as if his reasons should make sense and justify his actions. "You should get some of that for yourself. I'm sure he'd pay you—"

"Shut it!" Gabe's snarl verged on a roar, and Sofie began to cry.

Macky practically smothered the little girl with his comforting body, putting himself between her and any danger. Sniffling, the toddler pressed her face against the dog's floppy ear.

The visible shuddering of Gabe's chest betrayed his valiant struggle to get himself under control. His usual ice-man combat mode seemed to have deserted him. He'd confessed that his involvement with her and Sofie had become personal. Truth be told, their relationship—undefined as it was—had become personal to her too. And not just because she might well be dead and Sofie in her father's slimy clutches without Gabe's presence in their lives. Tara shook herself. No time to ponder feelings and attractions now.

She glared at Jimmy. "You've been in contact with Zander?"

"No, not directly. Um—ah, you know..." Jimmy's words trailed off into a wordless splutter.

The truth hit Tara like a freight train. "How long have you been on the payroll of Frazier's network?"

The man squirmed in his seat, as well he should.

"A while." The words escaped his lips in a whisper. Then his spine straightened as if he'd regained a measure of courage. "I'm going to pull this vehicle over. You can't shoot me because I'm driving, and we'll wreck. Then we'll see how well you do against Frazier's guys."

Snickering, Jimmy matched his actions to his words. The vehicle began to slow, and a glance behind them showed the van catching up.

"Get your foot off that brake." Gabe's words lashed the air. "I'm trained to shoot a flea off a fly's back. At this range, I'll have no problem plinking bits and pieces from your body that won't hinder your ability to drive. How do you feel about losing a pinky finger? And that's just for openers." He lifted the gun up far enough for the weapon to be visible in the rearview mirror to the driver.

"Okay! Okay!" The SUV sped up.

"This is what is going to happen." Gabe's icy operator tone continued. "You are going to hand your service weapon to Tara, butt first. Then you will give her your cell phone. Unlocked. Tara, when you have the phone, call the Casper office and tell them what's happened. The bad and the ugly, because there's sure not much good about our situation."

"Except we seem to have the upper hand."

"For the moment."

"Right." Her heart squeezed in on itself.

With a pair of dirty cops in the vehicle with them and a vanload of who knew how many on their tail, tenuous didn't begin to describe their situation.

"The Casper office needs to get a helicopter up here ASAP. At least by the time we reach the resort Bradley mentioned. If we can hold off that van behind us until then, they are likely to retreat in the face of a chopper-load of armed deputy marshals. And if not, they will probably be captured."

"Or worse." Tara nodded.

"Or worse." Gabe mimicked her nod.

At a wave of the gun in Gabe's hand, Dirty Deputy Jimmy complied meticulously with the instructions outlined, and Tara did the same. The ex-PJ knew what he was doing in fraught situations, and she could only be thankful for him in their lives. When she reached Tickner, genuine horror barked down the line from the head of the station, along with a pledge to dispatch the requested assistance immediately—a helicopter carrying a team from the US Marshals Service Special Operations Group.

As Tara ended the call and began to lower the phone, Brad lunged over the seat toward the gun in Gabe's hands. Apparently, he'd been exaggerating his disabled condition.

"I'm not going to prison." His shout rang through the cab.

Macky swiveled with a snarl, sharp teeth snapping a

hair's breadth from clipping off Brad's nose. The man subsided into the footwell of the passenger seat.

"Keep that creature away from me." He shielded himself with his hands, palms outward.

"Whether you get your face chewed on or not is up to you." Tara leaned forward and glared down at Brad. "Macky will do whatever is necessary to protect us. Isn't that right?" She patted the dog, who resumed shielding Sofie's tiny quivering body with his own. "Good boy." Tara lowered her head toward her niece. "Everything's going to be fine, sweetie."

Without looking, she fished inside the diaper bag at her feet and brought out the bear. The little girl cuddled the stuffed animal close and seemed to relax in her seat.

"How does it look with that van behind us?" Gabe asked the question without taking his attention from the driver.

Tara looked over her shoulder. "Whoever's at the wheel is keeping their distance about twenty feet back, not moving closer, but not falling back."

"Still hoping we're going to turn off and stop at some point, though they're probably plenty worried by now that the tables have turned." Gabe waggled the gun in Jimmy's direction. "Speed up. Go as fast as you can and still maintain safety."

"You're the boss." Sullenness dripped from the words.

"Don't forget it."

Tara checked over her shoulder again. "They're matching our speed, but I'd say we have a stalemate between them and us. With Sofie in the car, they don't dare open fire or ram us."

"Don't dismiss the possibility of some desperate act to achieve their boss's ends."

"I'll stay sharp."

Tara matched her actions to her pledge, regardless of the developing crick in her neck from maintaining focus over her shoulder. Likewise, she noted in her peripheral vision that Gabe's attention never wavered from the two traitorous deputies in the front seat.

Pregnant minutes crept past as their vehicle climbed higher through sharpening turns. They had to be nearing the mountain's summit. Tara's teeth ground together, and her insides twisted ever tighter. No audible or visible sign of the promised helicopter.

"They're moving closer." Her words emerged shrill and thin, as if her vocal cords had become taut wires.

"Hold steady." Gabe's firm voice admonished the driver as the SUV suddenly slowed, as if hoping to connect with the van behind.

Jimmy gave a grunt, and the vehicle sped up again.

The tree lines pressed in on them from either side. Walls of tall pines encrusted with deadfall and undergrowth. Tara swallowed against a claustrophobic sensation, as if the forest itself might fight on the enemy's side. She pushed the paranoid fancy away.

Help would be coming.

But what if no support arrived? What if they were on their own? Hadn't that been the way all along?

Gabe maintained his focus on the two lowlifes in the front seat. They constituted the danger inside the SUV. But he allowed his peripheral vision to take in the precious cargo by his side—Tara, Sofie and, of course, his faithful dog, Macky. Tara kept her gaze on the danger trailing them. Sofie cooed to her bear and made the stuffed animal dance on her lap, thankfully oblivious to the seriousness of the ongoing situation. Macky, as usual, guarded the baby. He stood alert, a pair of feet on either side of the hump bisecting the floorboard, dividing his attention between the toddler and the potential aggressors in the front.

The journey stretched on through a dim tunnel between thick stands of pine. Clouds hung low above them, enhancing the tunnel sensation. Then the gradient increased suddenly, and they burst free of the tree line into a rolling grandeur of rocks and native shrubs close at hand and the peaks of other mountains in the Laramie mountain range in the far vista. But the view was not what caused Gabe's sudden intake of breath.

The road widened, and several football fields' length away, a sprawling chalet-style resort with outbuildings nestled in the cleft of a pair of cliffs that led to the peak of the mountain. Snow capped the tallest spires soaring above the resort, but here, far south of Glacier National Park, the area remained snow-free. For now.

"The van is making a move on us." Tara's words were clipped.

"Go faster," Gabe told the driver.

Grumbling not nice words under his breath, Jimmy complied.

"They're going to catch us before we reach the resort." One hand lifting the gun confiscated from their driver, Tara whipped her head around to stare at Gabe with wide eyes.

Gabe glanced skyward. "Won't matter."

A steady thrum closed in on their location. Out of the clouds, a helicopter wearing the US Marshals Service insignia swooped down. Words poured from a bullhorn, commanding the van to halt. Gunfire spat from the ground, answered by a firestorm from the air.

Gabe didn't bother looking behind. "Get us to the resort. No stopping."

Tara let out a soft whoop. "The van's out of commission. Flat tires and steam pouring from the engine block."

A short few minutes later, at Gabe's direction, the SUV pulled up outside the resort's guest check-in door. Only half a dozen other cars sat in the large parking lot, but that number was not unusual at this lull between fall season activities—like hiking and four-wheeling to take in the striking colors and wildlife—and winter recreation—such as snowmobiling and skiing.

He glanced toward Tara. "Take Sofie and Macky inside. I'll wait here for the authorities to join us and scoop these two dirty deputies into custody."

She jerked a nod, expressive eyes telling him she saw the wisdom in his direction. With deft movements and comforting words for her niece, Tara unbuckled Sofie from the car seat and snatched up the diaper bag. As she opened the door and climbed out, her niece cuddled in her arms, brisk air—pure and piney, at this elevation—blew through the vehicle. About mid-thirties in temperature, Gabe estimated. Snow wouldn't be long in the offing. Tara shut the door and headed briskly for the reception area, the redbone coonhound trotting after them.

Driver Jimmy turned his head and glared at Gabe. The man's face was ashen. No doubt contemplating the dismal future of a law enforcement agent on the take.

"What sort of stake you got in this mess?" the man growled.

"Doing what's right."

Jimmy snorted. "What's right is reuniting a girl with her daddy."

"Even if that *dad* is the sort of scumbag you're supposed to arrest?"

The man shrugged. "Important for a kid to have a dad around."

"Biology does not a father make."

"What's that supposed to mean?"

"Would you two cut the philosophy discussion?" Brad inserted himself into the conversation. "Could I please sit up in the seat now?"

"Sure." Gabe peered into the front compartment to find the second dirty deputy still knotted into the footwell. "But when you turn, keep both your hands on the dashboard where I can see them at all times."

Brad snarled a few darkly creative words but complied.

A few minutes later, three heavily armed and armored members of the US Marshals Service Special Operations Group surrounded the SUV.

"Put down your weapons and come out of the vehicle with your hands up," an authoritative voice ordered.

As soon as Jimmy and Brad began to exit the SUV, moving like molasses in January, Gabe carefully placed the gun on the seat and got out with his hands in the air. All three of them were treated to being swung around and put into the frisking position, with their palms on the vehicle and their legs back and spread. Rough hands conducted a thorough search of their bodies. Gabe offered no resistance. The team was doing their job. Good guys would be sorted from bad guys soon enough.

Cuffs came out and started going on. As the chill metal began to close around one of Gabe's wrists, a crunch of approaching footsteps brought Hank Tickner into view.

The man laid a hand on the SOG member's shoulder as she was about to close the cuffs. "Not that one. He's with us."

The SOG member backed away, and Gabe offered a

grateful nod to the field office supervisor. The man returned the nod and motioned toward the building.

"Let's go inside out of the cold and see what we can figure out." He turned toward the hangdog pair of ex-deputies now in cuffs and scowled at them like they'd barfed on his shoes. What they'd actually done was worse. "Get these two out of my sight."

Gabe entered the resort with Tickner in his wake to find a vacant reception desk to their right and a spacious guest seating area to their left, populated with comfortable-looking rustic sofas and armchairs. Tara had taken off her jacket and was seated in one of the latter in front of a cozy fireplace containing a crackling blaze. Sofie, comfortably out of her snowsuit, sat on the rug at her feet, playing, while a contented-looking coonhound sprawled beside her.

Tara stood up as they approached. "Are they all in custody? No casualties?"

Tickner snorted. "Not unless you count the black eye to our office that those two disgraces to the badge gave us. Why were they taking you up this mountain, anyway?"

Gabe tensed and cast his gaze around the spacious lobby, narrowing his eyes at the entrances to hallways that led to unknown destinations and could hide enemies. Granted, this was the resort's off-season, but the place seemed too quiet, with employees conspicuously absent. Of course, the recent gunfire could well have driven the staff into hiding. But if that were the only reason for their absence, following the cessation of the gunfight, shouldn't they be emerging to investigate what was going on?

He frowned at Tickner. "I take it this resort was not the officially approved destination."

"The US Marshals Service would hardly run a safe

house out of a public resort." The man shot Gabe a disbelieving look.

Tara's hand closed convulsively over Gabe's forearm, and she joined him in scoping out their surroundings. "Then those bent deputies headed for this place for sinister reasons. It's not safe here. Zander's people must be waiting somewhere in this building to receive Sofie and carry her away."

Gabe turned toward Tickner. "We need to get out of here. Who knows how many of that crook's people he's got stashed around this place."

"Markson, get your warm things on and let's go." The supervisory deputy marshal snapped his fingers and moved toward the door, one hand going to the butt of the gun fastened to his belt.

"Chopper evac?" Gabe glanced toward the older man.

"You got it."

While Tara moved at high speed and Macky leaped to attention, Gabe's gaze never stopped roving the environment for threats that had yet to materialize. But his special operator senses were tingling off the charts. Maybe, just maybe, Zander's people were playing it cool with a SOG group in play outside, and their little band would be allowed to retreat without engagement. But they could assume nothing about Sofie's security, not to mention their own.

With Tickner forming a rearguard and shouting orders to the SOG group, they reached the US Marshals Service vehicle, which remained parked out front. Gabe swung open the rear hatch to retrieve their bags containing the firearms he itched to get his hands on. Tara dove into the back seat area, presumably to retrieve the child safety seat. As his fingers closed around the handles to draw the bags close, chaos erupted.

# TWELVE

Gritting her teeth, Tara wrenched the safety seat toward her while clutching Sofie and her ubiquitous diaper bag in her other arm. She backed away from the car. Bullets rained on the parking lot, originating from chalet windows, both upstairs and downstairs. Law enforcement personnel returned fire from cover behind the shot-up van and other vehicles in the lot.

Granted, the firefight was happening on the periphery on either side of where they were standing, and not directly at their location. But couldn't anyone get it through their heads to stop blasting away when a child was nearby? If only she could knock some skulls together. But the discipline was unlikely to pound any sense into the criminal element that had opened fire and was challenging the SOG team for control of the area.

Control of Sofie.

Tara hugged the child to her bosom. Let anyone try to rip the sweet, innocent girl away from her. She'd chew nails and spit tacks before that would happen.

A strong arm came around her shoulder. Gabe. He ushered her ahead of him toward the waiting helicopter. Each fist clutched a pistol, one his and one hers, which he'd pulled from their bags. Tara's arms were too laden to wield a weapon. Right now, her only defense was placing her body between her niece and the bullets spewing from the chalet. And Gabe positioned his body between them and the attackers in a stack formation, with Tickner as the caboose, actively returning fire on the criminal element.

The chopper sat only a few dozen yards away, and yet the time to get there seemed like an eternity of slogging through air weighted like mud and scented with an incongruous mix of heady pine and acrid notes of chemicals from discharged firearms. As they approached, a few bullets pinged off the body of the aircraft. The opposition's effort to disable the bird, no doubt. But the assault on the chopper trailed away and ceased as their little band neared the yawning doorway in the side of the sleek helicopter. Zander's people had to be under orders not to hurt Sofie and, likewise, the organized crime crew from the Frazier clan who had been drawn together in a symbiosis of allied goals.

Bitter bile rose in the back of Tara's throat. In that sense, the little girl's presence operated as a shield for the adults around her. An ironic circumstance that chafed like a burr caught in a sweater.

The closer they got to the US Marshals' bird, the stronger the downdraft of the whirling blades drove chill air spiked with pellets of dust into their faces. But Tara didn't falter a step. Nor did the men and the dog close on her trail. Thankfully, Sofie's face was buried in her aunt's jacket. The shudders of the little girl's body against hers gushed torrents of anger through Tara.

How unfair, how cruel that this child was forced to experience trauma after trauma perpetrated by the one man in the world who should willingly sacrifice anything, including his own custody of her, for his daughter's good.

But Zander Wolf didn't think that way. Never had. Likely, never would.

Tara reached the aircraft's body and flung herself and her precious cargo inside. Tickner and Gabe followed suit. The supervisory deputy marshal snatched the car seat from Tara and began buckling it into one of the seats, while Gabe situated his dog at the back of the bird and then joined Tara in settling Sofie into her harness. Tickner slammed the side door and began yelling at the pilot to "go, go, go." Even as they finished securing the child, the chopper leaped from the earth, and the adults half sat, half fell into available seats.

Breathing in great steam-engine gasps, Tara stared out into the parking lot, where the fight yet raged. A pencil-thin figure rushed from the resort's front doors, flanked by a pair of burly sidekicks. Frazier ran toward the helicopter, shooting a firearm and yelling something. The man's aim was so poor none of his bullets hit the helicopter, and the chopper's roar swallowed the sound of the man's words, but Tara had little doubt she read the man's lips all right.

*I want my car!*

Tara gasped at the sheer, self-centered audacity, as well as the oblivious mindset that seemed to assume he was either impervious to law enforcement bullets or no one would dare shoot him. The instant before the fleeing bird merged into the heavy cloud cover, Frazier appeared to trip and fall. More likely, cut down by one of the defenders on the ground. So much for the power of positive thinking when it came to invulnerability shields. Whether wounded or dead, the money launderer was likely done doing his dirty work. Funny how the thought brought meager comfort.

Scowling, Tara gripped the armrests in white-knuckled fists. "What about the SOG team?" Her voice emerged as a moderate shout. Even though the bird had evidently been built with noise-dampening features, the rotors still created a din. "There are only five of them, and who knows how many of the opposition hunkered down in the resort building."

A soothing hand gripped her tense shoulder. Gabe, who had the seat directly behind her. He'd been nothing but supportive throughout the ordeal, but right now she wasn't in the mood to be comforted.

Tickner, kitty-corner behind her, offered a nod of acknowledgment for her concern. "No worries. As we took off, I noticed our ground team vehicles moving into the lot. Plus, the SWAT team chopper from Casper PD is on the way. I trust our law enforcement to mop up."

Tara forced herself to stop trying to strangle the armrests. "Okay. Good to know."

"The important thing is getting you folks to a secure location."

"And where on God's green earth might that be?" Her scowl redoubled. "We've been searching for days, and every time we think we've found it, something blows our cover."

Her better nature admonished her worse self for the display of temper, but the pressure had built up until she had to blow.

Tickner seemed to borrow her scowl. "We can't go to the safe house we were originally going to use, because those two traitorous bozos with the Marshals Service would have told the crooks about it."

"Rent us an Airbnb." Gabe's advice came through as the voice of reason, as it had so often these past days. "Only don't charge it to the agency. Someplace remote, yet defensible."

He snapped his fingers. "Yeah, that might work. I could

assign a team to the perimeter, a deputy or two in the house, and—"

"Negative. Just me. I'll design the defenses."

"Who do you think you are?" The supervisory deputy's tone held a snarl.

"The guy who's had too much experience in situations where all but you and your own people are potential hostiles. Besides, how long can you keep that number of personnel committed to close-quarters protection?"

Tara gazed at Tickner, whose jaw worked like he were chewing on a bitter pill. Finally, he jerked a nod.

"One more thing," Gabe said. "You keep our location to yourself. No one in your office or anywhere in the Marshals Service can know where we are but you."

"Agreed."

"Have this bird put down in the nearest open parking lot to the rental garage where I stashed my truck."

Tara craned her neck around the seat to skewer Gabe with a glare. "Aren't you worried that the bad guys likely have a description and a license plate number for the truck, courtesy of Dirty Deputy 1 and Dirty Deputy 2?"

Gabe responded with an irritating smirk. "I'm counting on it. Relax. You'll see."

Something like a growl came from Tickner. "We need your statements to charge those deputies. If I turn you loose, how will we communicate?"

"Tara, would you give DD1's cell phone to Supervisory Deputy Tickner?"

*DD1? Oh, right, Dirty Deputy One.*

A reluctant grin spread over her face as she fished the captured cell phone from her pocket and gave it to Tickner.

He frowned at the device. "What's on here might help with the prosecution, but—"

"No worries." Gabe broke in. "I'm going to buy a pay-as-you-go phone ASAP. When I have it, I'll call you, and you can give us the address for the Airbnb. We'll get ourselves there—after I've done some essential shopping. As soon as we're settled, we'll give formal statements through whatever secure app your agency uses."

"Fair enough." The supervisory deputy nodded.

Exhaling the loudest huff she could manage, Tara turned around and faced toward the front of the chopper. The view out of the windshield had gone from opaque cloud cover to open spaces as they descended the mountain toward the city below.

She cast her attention toward Sofie, who'd been uncharacteristically silent throughout the flight. The little girl was fast asleep, slumped in her car seat with her head resting on her teddy. Tara allowed a small smile to curve her lips. To be so innocent as to pop off to sleep after a firefight and during an emergency helicopter ride. Tara's will firmed. She *would* preserve that innocence with every fiber of her being.

Of course, the personal pledge was good only as long as they defeated the threat to her niece's happy future. And that positive outcome seemed less likely every passing minute.

As soon as the US Marshals Service helicopter dropped them off in the vacant corner of a big-box store parking lot and then zipped away, Gabe tucked the child seat under his arm and led his little crew toward the storage facility a few blocks away. The highly unusual chopper landing had drawn attention, but as soon as they were out of sight of anyone who'd witnessed the drop-off, he made sure to keep their pace casual. Just like any other happy family out for a stroll.

*If only.*

They reached the facility without incident and without conversation. Tara's brooding silence, accompanied by gnawing her lower lip, betrayed her ongoing tension and troubled thoughts. Loading everyone into the sturdy old vehicle took only a few minutes, and then they were on the road, Gabe at the wheel.

"Plan?"

At Tara's one-word insistence on an explanation, Gabe offered her a grim smile. "First stop, a body shop for a quick-as-you-can truck makeover. Second stop, a big-box store for a pay-as-you-go phone, food and household supplies. Third stop, a hardware outlet for security gear and additional firearms. *Then* we call Tickner for directions to our final stop."

"Sounds like you have the operation planned, but—" An irritable squawk from Sofie interrupted whatever protest Tara was about to make. She let out a deep sigh. "My niece is hungry."

"You should have plenty of time to feed her while we wait at the body shop. While we're there, I'll go out for some sandwiches for us too. It's been a while since any of us has eaten."

"Let's do it."

Soon, a sign for a locally owned shop that did body work caught Gabe's attention. He turned the truck into the small lot. Dickering with the owner to abandon his current projects and get to work immediately on Gabe's took a few minutes and more than a few dollars, but soon he ushered Tara, a fussing Sofie and his dog into the small employee break room of the shop. Reluctantly, he left them seated around a scuffed table to get on with feeding the toddler while he walked up the block to a sub sandwich store. On the return trip, carrying warm subs and cool bottles of water, his pace picked up. Leaving his charges for even a few minutes had set his teeth on edge.

However, he needn't have worried. This time. Tara was just wiping Sofie's face and hands after the little girl's usual messy eating spree.

Upon his arrival, Tara swiveled in her seat and smiled at Gabe. His heart turned over. Women had smiled at him before—his mother, girlfriends, cashiers at store counters—all sorts of women. But never had his insides turned to warm goo at the flash of expressive eyes and the lovely face that lit up when he came into the room.

*Brother, you are in deep trouble with no way out, even if you wanted to escape.*

He thrust both the attraction and the unease over his feelings away. They had time only for business today. Well, and eating, which was an important kind of business also, because they needed to stay fueled and hydrated for the things that had to be done.

Time ticked away, the sandwiches were long consumed and Sofie was napping by the time the owner stepped into the break room, wiping his hands on a rag that smelled of grease and paint.

"All finished, sir. Can't say I've ever done a rush job like this before, but I hope you like the results."

Gabe, trailed by Tara, carrying Sofie, and Macky in the rear, followed the body-shop man into the spacious garage that held several work bays occupied by vehicles of various types.

Tara stepped up beside Gabe. She glanced around the area, then shot a questioning glance his way.

"Where's our truck?"

"Over there." Grinning, he pointed to a black Chevrolet pickup, the finish obscured by a dusting of Wyoming soil but sporting brand-new all-terrain tires that were likewise coated in dust. "Do you think anyone looking for a rust-specked white truck will pay any attention to this vehicle?"

"Not at first glance, but what about the license plates?"

Gabe turned toward the body-shop owner. "Did you fix that with a bit of mud to obscure a number or two?"

The man snorted. "Never have I had a customer insist on dirtying up a vehicle as soon as the paint was dry, but I'm not arguing with the bonus you're paying."

"Good." Gabe handed the man an extra hundred dollars. "That's for your discretion."

He grinned and stuffed the bills into a pocket of his oil and paint-stained coveralls. "You got it."

Gabe assisted Tara in buckling Sofie into her seat. The little girl roused slightly and let out a grumbly whine but then subsided into slumber again. The adults and the dog piled into the vehicle, and they left the body shop.

As they drove through the business district of Casper with the setting sun behind them, Tara frowned, but then she shrugged. "The license plate trick isn't strictly legal, but a minor infraction compared to the consequences of getting caught by Zander's people. I can live with it."

"That may be the literal truth." Gabe sent her a somber look.

"Granted."

"Let's get the phones and the supplies."

"Save that step until last. I need to stay in the vehicle while Sofie sleeps. You can pick up your security equipment. When you're done, hopefully she'll be ready to wake up, and we can shop for groceries and personal supplies together."

"Makes sense." Gabe guided the vehicle into a spacious parking lot and stopped the truck in a shadowed spot away from others. "I'll leave the truck running."

"Leave me a weapon, too."

"That and Macky." He handed her one of the pistols and got out of the pickup.

Scanning the area, Gabe spotted no threats, and his internal alarm system wasn't pinging—the sixth sense a lot of soldiers developed to a higher degree than a civilian, that just *knew* when a person was under hostile observation. Dusk had begun embracing the town in chilly arms. He shivered and zipped up his jacket as he strode toward the store's entrance.

Gabe worked through his mental shopping list as quickly as he was able, sometimes asking for assistance if he couldn't find something. Motion sensors, check. Trail cameras, check. *Hope everything's okay with Tara and Sofie. Head back in the game, buster. Tara is more than competent.* Wire filament, check. Camouflage netting, check. *This is taking too long. I need to get back to them. Neither of us even has a phone to call each other or to report an emergency. Take it easy. No rushing these things if you want to do them right.* Ammo for the pistols, lots of it, check. Vortex Razor HD LHT riflescope, check. Browning X-Bolt 2 Pro McMillan Carbon Fiber rifle with ammo, check. *These Western states sure make it easy to get good gear. I wonder if Tara, Sofie and Macky are doing all right out there. Why is this taking so long?*

Gabe looked at his watch and let out a long breath. He'd only been at this project for forty-five minutes and, by the looks of his cart, had made substantial progress. Yet, his unease had his breathing elevated and sweat beading his scalp. Maybe the case of uncharacteristic nerves stemmed from the fact that his little crew had been bouncing from one fraught situation to another for days on end. A respite felt…uncomfortable. Dangerous. Like his world was holding its breath for the next catastrophe.

Being out in the wild on military assignments had sometimes felt like this, too. So, what had he done, then? He stuffed his trepidation in a mental vault and did his job. Time to do the same. Swiping his brow with the back of his arm, Gabe pushed the cart up the aisle after the next item on his list.

Another half hour of intense shopping, followed by a quick trip through the checkout counter, and he finally wheeled a laden cart toward the spot where he'd parked the transformed pickup truck. His gaze scanned the lot, and his heart stumbled, then began to throb against his ribs.

One fact stood out above all others.

More vehicles had congregated in the area where he'd left the truck sheltering Tara, Sofie and his dog, but the slot where the vehicle had been stood empty.

# THIRTEEN

Despite keeping a close eye out for Gabe's approach, presumably with a shopping cart, she almost missed his dark figure moving like a panther through the night-shrouded parking lot. Only a sudden glint of light reflecting off the metal cart as it passed near one of the occasional streetlamps notified her of his approach. Then, suddenly, he halted and went stiff, head swiveling. Tara quickly turned on the truck's headlights and then doused them. If she weren't mistaken, the tension melted off his sturdy figure like wax that had met fire.

At a trot, he changed direction and pushed the cart toward their new position. Biting her lip, Tara let herself quietly out of the pickup to help him unload the gear he'd bought. She'd take whatever scolding he thought she had coming for nearly giving him a heart attack.

"Sorry about the confusion." She grabbed an item and placed it in the truck bed. "For some reason, people started parking up all around me, and it made me nervous not to be able to see a threat coming in time to stop it, so I moved the truck."

A wordless grunt answered her as Gabe practically threw his purchases into the pickup bed.

She grabbed his jacket sleeve and yanked, making him

look at her. A crescent moon kept his face mostly in shadow, but the compressed lips were easy to make out.

"I really am sorry. I would have called to warn you if I could have, but—"

"It's okay." The words came out gruffly, and then his sturdy arms wrapped around her, and she was crushed to his chest. "I understand. I was just scared. Um, terrified." An audible gulp punctuated the pronouncements.

Tara answered the squeeze with one of her own. Resting her head against him, she breathed in the odors of the outdoors on his jacket, as well as a little bit of dog and a lot of some pleasant, undefinable Gabe-scent that her heart had come to regard as synonymous with safety.

She lifted her head, and he let her go. "We'd better get a move on. There's more shopping to do."

"This time I'm not leaving you outside."

"And that's a fact. You're liable to get the wrong size of diaper if I let you go on your own."

Her small giggle was answered by a deep chuckle, and the heaviness between them dissipated. They climbed into the vehicle and headed out of the lot.

"Untraceable phones are a priority at our next stop," Gabe said. "Even ahead of diapers."

Tara grinned and rolled her eyes, though he couldn't see her reaction. "Not much in my life gets ahead of diapers these days."

As they proceeded to the next big-box store, the sense that their relationship had taken a profound turn lingered in Tara's mind. A new closeness, a deeper mutual understanding—whatever it was—warmed her insides like nothing had done in a long time. When this mess was all sorted out, and if Gabe asked her out on a date, would she go? In a heartbeat. But the very thought assumed they *would* defeat Zander in some final way that set them free. So far, she couldn't see their route to that outcome. *Please, God, help us.*

At the next store, they parked close to the entrance and piled out of the vehicle like a regular family. Sofie woke up without a fuss, so she must have had enough sleep for the time being, though the little girl's naps and nighttime slumbers had been disrupted all over the place in the past few days. Tara dreaded considering what that might mean for prospects of returning to routine at some point. Another problem for the nebulous future.

Within an hour, they had their phones, diapers, food and personal items squared away and in the truck. Once their little troupe had climbed in and buckled up, Gabe solemnly unwrapped his phone that had come with preloaded minutes.

"Go ahead and open yours also." Gabe handed her a device. "We should exchange numbers and get them plugged into our phones."

They accomplished that little chore quickly.

"Speaking of plugging in." Tara studied her cell's charge meter. "We need to get these devices more juice. I'm down to less than half a charge."

"First, we should call Tickner."

"I hope he's got a place for us to go."

"If not, we'll find one on our own. I'm tempted to do that anyway."

Tara shook her head. "I'd like at least one trusted person to know where we're at."

"Can't argue with you there." He began poking at his throwaway cell.

Soon, the sound of a ringing phone burred through the cab. Gabe must have put the call on speaker.

"Tickner here." A curt voice replaced the ringing. "Is this Gabe and Tara?"

"Got it in one." Gabe's tone was brisk. "Do you have a place for us?"

"I do. It's out of the city, and halfway up the mountain, but not so remote that you won't have cell service and modern conveniences. I'm not comfortable with you being totally incommunicado."

"Neither am I," Tara spoke up. "What's the status on the arrestees from the resort incident?"

The supervisory deputy gave a wry chuckle. "At the moment, it's controlled chaos. Not quite like herding cats, but almost. The perps are currently vying with each other for the best deal for the fastest talk. Some of them are saying they were hired by proxy for some 'dude hiding out in another country.'"

"Zander Wolf."

"No doubt," Tickner confirmed Tara's pronouncement. "The other group is blaming Frazier for roping them in on a 'stupid personal problem' that had nothing to do with business."

"Sounds like a good thing to have these resentments loosening tongues."

"It is, but a couple of the perps took law enforcement bullets and are in the hospital, which, as you know, creates mountains of paperwork and baskets of procedural hoops to jump through. At least none of our people was killed, though a couple have minor wounds."

"Frazier?" Gabe's one-word query drew an indrawn breath from Tickner.

"Now, that's an interesting one. He didn't get a scratch from law enforcement, but he was howling that it was our fault that he tripped, fell down, skinned his knee and get this—ruined a pair of designer jeans that could pay one of our quote-unquote 'bargain-basement Fed salaries for a month.' That was hour one in custody. Now, well into hour three, we already have early signs that things are not going to go well for the smug joker."

"How so?" Gabe asked.

"We've got him dead to rights, with multiple law enforcement witnesses, shooting at a US Marshals Service helicopter carrying three deputy marshals—pilot included—a civilian and a child. Frazier can hire the most expensive lawyer on the planet and not wiggle out of a conviction on multiple counts of attempted murder. He's had his phone call, and guess what? No one from the juggernaut law firm that usually defends organized crime members from his loose consortium has leaped into their limo to race to his defense. If I'm reading the situation right, his criminal buddies are in the process of distancing themselves from him and will soon install a replacement money launderer."

Tara gusted a soft laugh. "He's not as untouchable as he assumed he was."

"Not when you attract the kind of attention he's drawn by throwing a tantrum over a car."

"A vehicle he was never going to get his grubby pinkies on." Gabe snorted. "What about our charming pair of dirty deputies?"

A beat of silence fell, then Tickner huffed. "That's a good question. They've both clammed up and lawyered up, but the district attorney is ready to forge ahead with charging them because a couple of Wolf's people from the van that was following you are maintaining they were told the Casper office deputies in your car had been paid to hand you over. But to really make the charges stick, we need statements from the two of you."

A beep from the device in Gabe's hand signaled a low charge.

Gabe frowned at the cell phone. "We'll have to let you go as soon as you give us the address for the Airbnb, but you'll have our statements via a secure online app first thing in the morning."

"I'll hold you to that. Here's the address, and here's how to get there since you don't have GPS in that truck."

Tara listened closely and committed the location to memory. Gabe ended the call and reached for the stick to put the truck in gear.

She laid a hand on his arm. "One more thing before we head up the mountain. I need to check on the status of my partner."

"Call your office in Great Falls?"

"Nope. I'm going to go to the source of the latest and best—Brennan's wife."

"You know her number by heart? Most folks just keep those things in their contacts list."

"Fun fact." Tara chuckled. "Lisa's number is only one digit different than my regular phone that we left at your place. We used to laugh about that oddity at coworker gatherings—you know, the odd summer barbecue or birthday party."

"Go for it."

Stomach knotting at what she might find out about her critically injured partner, Tara tapped in the digits. The phone rang and rang. Would Lisa pick up, and if not, what did that mean? Then came a faint click, as if someone had answered.

"Lisa?"

No words in response, just rustling and then a ringing like someone else's nearby phone had been called.

"Hello, Tara. I believe you have someone who belongs to me."

The mellifluous voice played chills along her vertebrae as if her spine were a xylophone.

"Zander?" The word dripped faintly from her lips like a meager drop of water falling into an ocean.

Gabe's whole body went rigid. Even his teeth ground against each other.

"What? How?" Tara choked a little. "Where is Lisa? What have you done to her?"

"Relax." Zander let out a slimy chuckle. "Your partner's loving wife is fine, just missing her phone. We appropriated it because we figured you'd call her number for an update on dear, brave Brennan sooner or later."

"Don't you say that good man's name on your twisted lips."

Tara's ferocity set Gabe's hair on end. Good thing for the lowlife at the other end of the call that he wasn't within her arm's reach.

"I'd think you would have learned by now that I do what I want when I want." The man's voice went arctic.

"How is that working out for you so far?" Gabe didn't even try to keep the taunt out of his tone. "Despite some concerted effort, Sofie's still right where she's supposed to be—with her aunt."

"Ah, would that be the washed-up special operator?"

"Better than a murderous con man who deludes himself that the fake looking back at him in the mirror is a worthy parent."

"Who do you think you are?" Heat boiled from the outburst. "Some daddy-wannabe?"

Gabe's insides cringed. *Was* he starting to think he'd

like to be Sofie's dad? He tamped the thought down and swallowed the sting. He wasn't about to let this guy know he'd scored a hit.

"I could answer with some classic Rambo, like being your worst nightmare. But the truth is, *you're* the nightmare, and it's about time someone gave you a wake-up call."

Tara leaned her face close to the phone. "You listen to me, you cheap disgrace. You killed my sister—Sofie's mother. And now you want to kidnap your own daughter. The courts gave *me* custody of her, not you, so crawl back into whatever hole you've been hiding in and stay there."

"Courts?" Wolf barked a laugh. "In my world, blood is thicker than the law."

"In my world, the law is going to squash you like a bug."

Tara's finger jammed the End button as if she were doing some squashing herself. The harshness of her heavy breathing dominated the truck cab.

"What was that all about?" She ran the splayed fingers of her hands through the thick hair at the top of her head.

"Intimidation."

"Yeah, well, he succeeded in baiting the mama bear."

"I'll vouch for that." Gabe released a clipped chuckle. "I suspect he had something he wanted to say, but you didn't let him get to it. He's probably gnashing his teeth at the lost opportunity."

"I need to let my Great Falls office know that some Zander henchman has Lisa's phone. They'll cut the line off right quick." She lifted the device as if to tap in a number, but a ping notification indicated she had a text message.

Gabe leaned over her to see the screen as she opened the message. Call me when you're ready to be reasonable. A number followed the words.

"Reasonable?" Tara snorted. "The man doesn't know the meaning of the word."

"Chuck the phone."

Tara stared at him, wide-eyed.

"Just throw it out the window. The device will either be smashed by a vehicle driving over it or picked up by a stranger and carted off to who knows where. Either way, the cell won't trace to you, now that they have the number."

She inhaled a long breath and let it out slowly. "Good idea. I don't want Zander's contact information anyway." In synchronized motion, she pressed the button to lower the window with one hand and tossed the device like a Frisbee with the other.

"No worries about the number. I memorized it. We should pass the information along to the authorities here and in Great Falls."

"For all the good knowing his number will do. The call no doubt originated in the Maldives. Non-extradition, remember?"

"You never know when intel will come in handy in surprising ways." Gabe put the truck in gear. "Make your calls to the supervisory deputies with my phone." He passed her the device. "Let's go home. Well, at least our temporary home away from home."

As he drove, he listened to the calls on speakerphone between Tara and Tickner in Casper, as well as Henderson in Great Falls. Both supervisory deputies were happy to get Zander Wolf's contact number, even though triangulating a location would not lead to an arrest of someone living in a non-extradition country.

Henderson reassured Tara that Brennan and his wife, Lisa, were both fine. In fact, Brennan had emerged from his coma and seemed alert, recognizing the people around him. However, the head wound had erased his memory of the days prior to his injury. The damage had also limited his ability to speak and affected the fine motor skills on one side of his body. Medical staff were hopeful that, with therapy, he would recover much of his function, though they weren't sure that the memory of the gunfight that saw him injured would return. Such loss of recall around a traumatic event was common, especially with a head wound.

Tara ended her calls, and Gabe felt her eyes on him. He offered her what he hoped was a reassuring smile.

She bit her lower lip and shook her head. "I didn't have the heart to ask whether the prognosis included an eventual return to work as a deputy marshal. A close second to his family, Bren lived for the job."

Gabe reached out and gave her hand a quick squeeze. "An issue beyond your control. Such a trauma will no doubt have your partner reevaluating his life, but what he chooses to do as a result is up to him."

"And Lisa."

"For sure."

Tara hugged herself and sighed. "I apologize for my negativity when I've just been given good news about Brennan's survival. I'm just feeling…bereft. So much loss in people's lives, including my life and in Sophie's, all at the hands of one supremely selfish and self-centered man."

"Hang in there. The story's not over yet."

Tara went silent, staring down at her lap. Gabe left her alone to ruminate. She had a lot to process.

Thirty minutes later, they pulled into a gravel parking space adjacent to a charming A-frame cabin with gingerbread trim and a three-sided deck. The small structure could be reached by vehicle only by bumping slowly along a lengthy narrow driveway. A forest of spruce, pine and aspen surrounded the cabin. but Gabe noted with appreciation that the tree line stood at least fifty feet away from the dwelling on all sides. Hostiles would have to step into the open for a considerable distance to reach the building. Further details would have to wait until daylight to evaluate.

"Wait here." Gabe made a halting motion toward Tara with his hand. "I know Sofie's hungry, fussy and probably needs a change, but I'm going to apply the door code Tickner gave us and scout the inside first."

"Understood."

Crisp night air bit at Gabe's nose and cheeks as he approached the dark doorway with his pistol in hand. The building showed no sign of life and was almost certainly empty, but he winced as a porch board creaked under his boot. At the door, he halted and listened. Silence from the home, an owl hooting from the woods.

The buttons for the digital door lock beeped faintly under his fingers. Gabe stepped in and automatically slid to the side along the wall, so as not to present a target backlit by the pale moonlight. Not a dust mote stirred at his smooth insertion. The interior of the cabin was warmer than the exterior, but he'd definitely need to turn the heat up during their occupancy. Tension ebbed from Gabe's shoulders. There is a specific type of feeling to a structure that is truly void of warm-blooded presence. As a veteran of clearing hostile spaces, Gabe was well familiar with that feeling. His little crew was alone here.

But just to make sure, he hazarded a click of a wall switch and found himself in a compact living area with a couch and two easy chairs facing a wood-burning fireplace. The air smelled faintly of cozy fires past. A dining table sat behind the couch with a galley kitchen to the right, as well as a hallway. The hallway brought him to a bathroom-cum-utility-room on one side and a bedroom on the other. He returned to the living room and let his gaze travel up the stairs along one wall to find a loft with the edges of a bed showing beyond wooden rails. For Sofie's safety, the loft would need to be his, but come morning, he would secure the single window in the small first-floor bedroom against intruders.

Gabe stepped outside and motioned for Tara to come in. She did so quickly with Sofie, Macky and the ever-present diaper bag in tow. Gabe set about unloading the food and comfort supplies and left them on the kitchen peninsula counter while Tara looked after her niece. Then he brought in what defensive equipment he'd purchased that could possibly be damaged overnight by the cold weather outside. He stored those items in a hideaway closet he discovered under the stairs.

As he began to stow perishables in the refrigerator and freezer, Tara stepped out of the downstairs bedroom, her expression as relaxed as he'd seen her look all day. Sofie rode in the crook of her aunt's arm, and she, too, appeared in a better mood. Macky, standing at Tara's side, just looked like himself.

"This is nice." Her gaze swept the open main area. "Cozy, but nice."

"I agree. I think we can all be comfortable here. Tomorrow, though, I'm going to do everything in my power to make us as safe as possible. But for now, how about some canned beef stew with French bread?"

Tara grinned at him, and Gabe's heart did its usual flip whenever she lit up like that. He turned away, searched for and found the pots-and-pans cupboard. Sofie wiggled to be let down, and as soon as Tara set her on her feet and released her, the toddler got busy exploring her new environment under Macky's watchful eyes. Tara found the can opener for the stew and then began slicing and buttering thick slabs of bread. Gabe started humming an Eagles tune, and Tara chimed in with the words in a lovely alto. Just like that, they were a happy family enjoying peaceful domesticity.

*If only.*

But now was not the time to douse the mood with doubts. Plenty of time for second thoughts and caution tomorrow. And the next day. And the next. However long they were allowed this respite from attack.

At dusk on the second day, Gabe was standing outside on the porch, nursing a steaming cup of coffee, while he watched the sun dip its rays into the trees.

Tara stepped outside to stand by him. "You've done a great job shoring up the defenses around here."

Gabe glanced at her. "A part of me was enjoying the sunset, while another part was wondering what else I could do to secure the property."

He'd had a busy time posting trail cameras in every direction, alarms on the perimeter and covering his truck with camouflage netting so it would be hard to spot from the air. Every window had been covered with heavy-duty aluminum screens—the type that would require some sort of cutter to get through and access the glass. When they left the property, Gabe would remove the screens and repair any nail holes in the sills. Until then, he needed to cut off or delay any attack opportunities offered by unprotected windows.

He'd also installed upgraded deadbolts on the front and back doors, and every night he stuck chairs under the knobs, an unsophisticated but effective blockage. However, the deadbolts and chairs were deployed only after he strung cans on ropes all around the porch rails at dusk, a cheap low-tech alarm. If intruders reached the building unseen, they'd certainly be heard soon enough to offer a few seconds' response time from the defenders. Would the warning be enough? Gabe slept with his gun under his pillow. He knew Tara did the same.

She looked up at him, and his heart lurched at the desolation in her eyes.

"You've been wonderful to Sofie and me from day one." Tara abruptly turned away, showing him a hunch-shouldered back. "I've been thinking about the situation continually while you've been working like a dynamo to stop the unstoppable, and I've reached a conclusion." She squared her shoulders and faced him. "I'm done. This life on the run is not good for Sofie, or for any of us. There is only one way to make the attacks stop—offer to give my niece to her father."

Gabe staggered backward. She may as well have punched him in the mouth. Tara Markson and surrender didn't belong in the same sentence. Maybe he had misunderstood her. But no, the hardness in every plane of her face telegraphed that she meant each word of what she'd said.

# FOURTEEN

Under other circumstances, Gabe's shocked reaction might have been funny, but now her gut wrenched. He needed to understand and support her this one last time.

Tara stepped forward and gripped his upper arms in her hands. "We need to make Zander Wolf return to the US in person. If I offer to hand his daughter over, but only to him face-to-face, no third party, I believe he's arrogant enough to think he can slip in and out of the country."

"But the invitation will be a trap." Comprehension lit Gabe's eyes. "Won't he suspect he's being set up?"

"Of course. We'll have to outmaneuver him."

He frowned as a faraway look settled over his face. Tara could practically see the wheels turning in his head.

"Wolf has shown himself resourceful and ruthless. We would have to think like him to catch him. I don't think either of us has that level of disregard for others."

"We don't have to *do* as he would do. Just put ourselves in that mindset so we can envision how to counter or even forestall his moves."

"4D chess. I hate the risks, but I see the necessity. With great reluctance, I have to admit you may have hit on the only viable way to end the attacks permanently."

"Then, you'll help me."

His hazel eyes glinted green. "Always."

"Then let's get busy planning."

"I assume we need to involve law enforcement in whatever we devise."

"Only a trusted few. DD1 and DD2 have shown me how vulnerable even my own agency is to corruption. And Zander is a master corrupter."

"Understood." Gabe nodded. "Where do you want to do this fake exchange?"

"Here. Right in this location where you've already got excellent defenses set up."

"We'll have to let him inside those defenses if we're going to pretend to give him Sofie. And I don't think he'll come alone."

"I'm counting on a level of havoc that will conceal our activities."

Gabe snorted. "Now we just have to figure out what those activities will be. I—" From somewhere on his person, a cell phone rang, cutting off whatever he was going to say.

Tara leaned her back against the deck railing while he unzipped his jacket and reached into his shirt pocket. He looked at the screen, frowned and handed the device to her.

"I think your boss wants to talk to you."

"Henderson?" She consulted the screen and recognized the name that she'd entered into the contacts on their shared phone only two days ago. Her breath caught. Had Brennan taken a turn for the worse? She thumbed the answer button. "Hello? Everything okay at your end?"

"We lost him." Henderson barked the words.

"What? Brennan?" Her pulse rate skyrocketed.

"No. Wolf. His phone just went dark."

"So, Bren's all right."

"Of course, your partner's okay. Wolf's gone."

Why was her boss sounding so brusque? Zander must have turned off the phone attached to the number he'd given her. They'd located its origin in the Maldives, for all the good the knowledge gave law enforcement in the US. Then her heart clenched. What if she'd waited too long to get back to the louse? What if he never turned that phone on again? How would she contact him to set the baited hook? Their plans would be for nothing.

Tara's shoulders slumped. "Zander must have decided I wasn't going to call him back and either turned off or discarded the phone."

"We don't think so."

"What do you mean?"

"An FBI contact in the Maldives says Zander Wolf's private plane left the country twenty hours ago."

Tara studied Gabe's grim face as she gnawed her lower lip. "Any idea where the guy is headed?"

"The flight plan says Tijuana, Mexico."

"Good." She straightened up, no longer leaning on the deck rail. "He can be apprehended and extradited from there."

Henderson's heavy sigh didn't bode well. "Only if he lands where he says he's going to land."

"He's coming to the US." Gabe injected the comment into the conversation with an air of certainty. "He's done waiting for his goals to be achieved by third parties. Done trusting others to succeed. Zander Wolf is on the hunt with a deeply personal goal."

"The FBI and we at the US Marshals agree on that, but we have no idea where this guy's plane will land. Other than somewhere in the northwest and clandestinely at an obscure airport, for certain. And we're worried about something else."

"What's that?" Dread sank claws into Tara's heart. She had a bad feeling about what her boss was going to say.

"Knowing this guy, he's not going to be satisfied with reclaiming his daughter. He's going to want to eliminate the people who have stood in his way for so long."

Tara locked stares with Gabe.

"I agree." He nodded. "Wolf won't want to leave Tara alive and capable of trying to get Sofie back. Me, either, because I've been such a burr under his saddle. Tara and I were just talking about putting ourselves in his mindset so we could anticipate his next move. Hopefully entice him to come here personally. Apparently, he's already on that path. Now we have to be ready to outsmart him when he comes at us."

"Is that all?" Henderson snorted. "This guy is as tricky as a tarantula, stealthy as an owl and dangerous as a rattler hiding under a cactus."

Tara's grip tightened around the phone. "How soon do you predict Zander will be in-country?"

"Tonight possibly, but sometime tomorrow for sure."

"Do you think he knows where we're keeping Sofie?"

Gabe folded his arms across his chest. "I don't think he'd be on his way if he didn't have some idea."

"Concur," Henderson said. "We'll get a small army of deputies up there tonight. A few FBI agents, too, if I read their level of engagement right."

"Negative." Gabe shook his head. "You do that, and he'll know exactly where we are in a heartbeat. You'll lead him right here."

"Yeah, but he won't be able to get through us to get to you."

"So, maybe he'll just go away?" Tara rapped her heel against the porch boards. "For how long? Chasing him off will leave me—and now it's been Gabe and me—living constantly on high alert and ready to run at any moment. I've already decided I can't live that way any longer, and the instability is not good for Sofie. No, we need to catch this guy and put him out of the picture."

"Well, sure, that would be optimal, but—"

"How about this?" Gabe gently pried the phone out of her rigid fingers, and she let him take it. "Don't rush in here with a large group of people looking as conspicuous as a dog at a cat convention. Coordinate with Tickner and have a Special Operations Group on alert in the area. Get them up here in the woods doing exercises, maneuvers or whatever, but not too close to us. Just near enough that when we alert, they can reach us within minutes. We need to look enticingly vulnerable."

Tara leaned over the phone. "The goal here, sir, is not only to protect Sofie but to eliminate the threat. If that means accepting elevated risk, that's what must be done."

"Very well." Henderson's curt tone had returned. "If you're ready to go on the offense while looking defenseless, the US Marshals Service will support you all the way."

"Can you get the FBI to hold off?"

"I'll certainly try. Let me make a few phone calls, and I'll get back to you."

"Good. We're almost ready at our end. Gabe has been doing amazing security things all over the property. I don't think a bunny rabbit could sneak up on us."

She grinned up at him, and a flush crept up his neck, deepening the red that the crisp fall breeze had painted on his cheeks.

"I'll do my best to live up to your faith in me." The words came out somewhat strangled.

Tara sobered. She enjoyed teasing this guy, but defeating Zander and ensuring Sofie's safety didn't allow room for levity. With the murderous man her sister had called husband mere hours away, neither she nor Gabe would be getting any sleep tonight.

How did that old saying go? I can rest when I'm dead?

*Please, God, don't let that become a true saying for Gabe, Sofie or me. I'm sorry for not trusting You with my life and hers. From this moment, I'm letting You be in charge. And Gabe, too. I've seen You using his knowledge and training to work on our behalf.*

"Let's get cracking."

Gabe's brisk words pulled Tara from her silent prayer. She hadn't even noticed that the phone conversation with her boss had ended. But the internal epiphany had been worth the distraction. In her heart, something basic had changed. Whatever happened, she now knew God was with her. With them.

Measuring each footfall, Gabe glided through the midnight forest. He'd ventured out well beyond the perimeter of the alarms and traps he'd set as he made a circuit around the cabin where Tara waited, armed and standing guard over a slumbering Sofie, with Macky there alongside them. The coonhound's ears and nose ensured an accurate early warning system. But Gabe felt he needed to personally scout the few approaches within a mile of their location that would offer spots for one or more vehicles to park and disgorge hostiles.

The trees around him shushed gently in the cool breeze. Thankfully, the weather had taken a turn for the warmer.

Though the wee hours of the night were upon them, the temperatures remained above freezing, and clouds from his breath were not going to give his presence away. Of course, that meant others would not be betrayed by the condensation, either. He needed to rely mostly upon his ears to discern an alien presence.

So far, normal forest noises continued. A nearby rodent rustling beneath the carpet of fallen pine needles. An owl hooting in the distance. And then—Gabe froze where he stood and strained his hearing.

There was something…yes, a faint, rhythmic popping noise, like tires crawling slowly over gravel. A vehicle approached. No, two. The slightly staccato rhythm of the popping betrayed a second vehicle. The lack of engine purrs suggested electric cars or SUVs of some sort—the kind of vehicles bad actors might choose to sneak up on a location. Who else would be moving so stealthily through the night with lights off?

Gabe stood rock-still, cradling his rifle, at the edge of a clearing that verged a low-maintenance gravel road. He remained shielded from view by the boughs of a spruce tree but could see between the branches into the grassy space. Unless he missed his guess, the middle-of-the-night intruders would park here, get out and slink toward the cabin on foot.

The next moments proved he'd surmised correctly. Hulking dark forms turned off the road, one after another, and stopped at the edge of the trees. Gabe could hardly tell when the silent engines turned off. Then eight doors swung open almost simultaneously, with no interior lights flashing on. He glimpsed the same number of bodies—mere shadows in the faint moonlight—exit the vehicles.

Gabe remained still, his heart rate low and steady, his

breathing deep and even. One with his surroundings. Even if this group included trained wilderness fighters, they were unlikely to detect his presence, since he was already here when they arrived. There was no sound, no motion, no minute stirring of the air that could alert the most sensitive among them.

To err on the side of caution, Gabe allowed himself only peripheral vision to study the new arrivals. A direct, steady stare had been known to tickle the awareness of individuals sensitive to surveillance—a well-documented but poorly explained human phenomenon.

Stray moon-glints off metallic objects betrayed weapons in hands that appeared to be covered by thin black gloves. The eight dark-clad figures were either wearing balaclavas or, unless their skin was naturally dusky, had blackened their faces artificially. Yet another sign these people were up to no good. As if he'd doubted their intentions for a moment. Which figure in this group was Zander Wolf? Impossible to know.

Low-voiced conversation reached Gabe's ears.

"Spread out and proceed due north." The male voice oozed command. "When we reach the cabin, surround it, and wait for my signal."

Zander? For some reason, the timbre didn't match what he remembered from the man's brief conversation with Tara. But then the guy was barely speaking above a whisper, so the voice wasn't a solid identifier.

The urge to attack this group, to keep them away from Tara and Sofie, swept through Gabe, threatening to ramp up his pulse rate and breathing. He ruthlessly tamped down the impulse. At this point in the proceedings, he'd only get himself killed.

*Stick with the plan, dude.*

His body listened to the inner admonishment and remained in stasis, even as stealthy dark figures began to penetrate the woods around him. One guy passed within feet of Gabe and gave no sign of sensing his presence.

Gabe held himself still for one minute, and then two. Finally, he allowed motion and crept silently into the clearing. Drawing his field knife from a sheath at his waist, he knelt beside each tire on the two vehicles and stabbed them. Escaping air hissed into the night, and the vehicles settled on their tire rims. Whatever happened, the hostiles were not escaping by the same means by which they arrived.

He allowed himself a grin as he melted once more into the trees and began to tail his first target, who was unlikely to be checking his six when all his intel told him the resistance lay ahead. A huge mistaken assumption. A mistake Gabe had learned the hard way not to indulge during his first mission in the military years ago.

Soon, the snap of a twig under a careless foot, accompanied by a stumble and a faint curse, alerted Gabe that his quarry was near. At least some of these guys were not experienced woodsmen, making his task marginally easier, but no less perilous. One lapse in judgment and he could take a bullet that would no doubt set off a firestorm from the rest of the criminal crew. Then he'd better not make a mistake.

On noiseless feet, Gabe came up behind the sneaking gunman and slammed the butt of his rifle against the back of the guy's head. The man dropped like a stone, out cold, and with minimal sound. Gabe got to work with zip ties and duct tape, and soon this potential combatant had been rendered null and void.

One down, seven to go.

Gabe moved onward, now traveling obliquely from his former position to intercept another hostile. This one seemed more attuned to his surroundings and possessed superior tradecraft to his comrade. Gabe hung back, barely keeping the soundless shadow in sight, and only moving when the man moved, though at a slightly faster pace. The distance between them began to lessen.

But something must have alerted the mercenary to enemy presence, because the man suddenly whirled, starting to bring up his rifle. Gabe was near enough that the move only meant the guy took the rifle butt to the face rather than to the back of the skull. Same result. Soon, this hostile was out of action, too.

Gabe moved on, urgency riding his gut. They must be getting close to the cabin now. Time to make some noise, so Tara would know to notify the SOG team to close in.

He closed in on a third attacker. "Hey, buddy," he whisper-called.

The man whirled and dropped low all in one motion like an experienced fighter. However, he pulled the trigger a bit too soon. Gabe did not. The gunman's bullet thunked into a nearby tree, while he went down, howling, a bullet in his knee. However, Gabe couldn't fault him for attempting to bring his gun to bear again. He strode forward and kicked the rifle from the man's grip, following that kick with a second one to the guy's face that laid him out groaning.

At the near-simultaneous gun blasts, bedlam rent the night. Someone tripped the wire that activated the strobing floodlights mounted on the cabin roof, effectively blinding and disorienting approaching attackers and eliminating any possibility of sneaking across the open area unseen. A few yards away, someone stepped in a snare and let out a high-pitched shriek as he flipped skyward, dangling upside down by one foot. But apparently, he didn't lose his grip on his rifle because he started blasting away in random directions.

Crouching low beneath the wild shot, Gabe moved closer, then plinked the rifle out of the guy's grip, winning another pained howl as the mercenary cradled a bloodied hand and swung back and forth helplessly in the night breeze.

*Tara, I hope you've called the cavalry, because there are still four guys out here.*

Even as the hope passed through his mind, gunfire from multiple rifles hosed down the front of the A-frame. Tinkling glass betrayed that bullets had slipped through the mesh and into the house. A chill pierced Gabe's heart. Sofie was safe in the back bedroom, but Tara was likely in the living room where the attack was concentrated. He needed to distract these mercs' attention.

Taking a knee at the edge of the tree line, Gabe brought his Browning rifle to his shoulder and began answering the gunfire wherever barrel sparks lit the night. In short order, the attackers discerned his position and began returning fire. Gabe rolled away, changed his position and returned to steadily firing his weapon. Someone in the cabin was doing the same. Warmth spread through Gabe's chest. Tara. She must be alive and well.

*Thank You, God.*

Something like a hot fist slammed into the outside of Gabe's left shoulder, knocking him flat. Wet warmth spread across his upper arm, but no pain. Yet. Adrenaline held that at bay for now. He lifted his arm. Yes, it still worked. The injury couldn't be too severe then, but he had no time for further assessment as more bullets thwacked trees around him. Gabe rolled away from his former position, grunting as pain suddenly bit when his weight momentarily pressed the injured limb against the ground.

*Anytime, SOG. We're ready for your help.*

As if the thought conjured the armed response team, fresh gunfire split the night from different caliber rifles than the mercs were using.

"Drop your weapons," an authoritative voice bellowed from the woods behind the attackers. "You're surrounded by a United States Marshals Service Special Operations Group, and you're under arrest."

All guns fell silent. Then grunts, rustles and curses spelled bad guys being taken into custody.

Gabe lowered his rifle and came to his feet, calling out and identifying himself. The team leader came out to meet him in the yard, and Gabe told him about the subdued mercs deeper in the woods.

The front door of the cabin swung tentatively ajar. "Everything copacetic out there?"

"Yes, ma'am." The team leader moved toward the cabin, and Gabe followed.

"Do you have Wolf?"

"Identities haven't been sorted yet, but everyone out here has been apprehended, so I must assume so."

Tara snorted as she stepped outside, Macky flanking her. "Assume nothing where Zander is concerned."

Gabe climbed the stairs onto the deck and drank in Tara's glowing health despite the haggard look in her eyes. Macky, too, looked whole as his tail practically wagged off his rear end. They'd been through a lot in a few fraught days, but maybe the frenzy was finally over.

Tara's gaze settled on him, and her eyes went wide. "You're injured." She pointed toward his arm.

Gabe glanced down at his shoulder and found a crimson stain growing across his jacket sleeve. "I don't think the wound is too serious. A graze or possibly a through-and-through, but no bones broken."

Tara's lips thinned. "We need to stop the bleeding." She grabbed his uninjured arm and guided him into an Adirondack chair.

"No worries, Deputy Markson." The team leader lifted a radio from his belt. "I'll get our medic over here while you check on anyone remaining in the cabin."

"Good idea." Tara jerked a nod, sent Gabe a concerned look. "I'm shocked Sofie's not wailing her head off with startlement from all the noise out here."

She disappeared into the house as the medic climbed the stairs, toting a small kit. He got to work treating what turned out to be a deep bullet graze.

Shortly, another man approached the porch wearing a grim look. "Wolf isn't among the mercs."

"What?" Gabe leaped to his feet.

Tara burst through the cabin's front door, her eyes frantic. "This whole frontal assault was a distraction. Someone cut through the mesh over the bedroom window in the back, and Sofie's gone!"

Gabe's heart hit his toes. They'd planned like generals and fought like tigers, but they'd still failed to protect the vulnerable innocent who depended on them.

# FIFTEEN

Shaking in every limb, Tara lunged toward the deck stairs, but a strong arm wrapped around her and pulled her back. She wriggled around and punched blindly, connecting with something solid, but vulnerable. Gabe's sharp hiss focused her. She'd struck him on his injured shoulder.

She looked up into Gabe's drawn face. "I'm sorry. I am. But I have to go get her."

"*We* will go get her."

"You're wounded."

"Obviously. But not so badly we can't put Macky on the scent and run down a Wolf."

The fight ebbed from Tara's body. "What if he reaches a vehicle? What if—"

Gabe's finger pressed against her trembling lips.

"I disabled the vehicles. He's on foot until he contacts someone to come get him or steals something."

The SOG leader stepped forward. "I'll get the US Marshals Service chopper in the air. It has infrared capability. We'll see anything in the area alive on the ground."

Gabe nodded. "Do it."

"And I'll get my jacket and handgun to go with my rifle." Tara freed herself from Gabe's arms, immediately missing the measure of comfort they had provided. Enough so that she'd gathered herself again.

"Bring Sofie's teddy." Gabe tilted his head toward the cabin. "Macky probably doesn't need the exposure after being around you all for days, but he can refresh himself on the scent by smelling Sofie's favorite toy. Oh, and grab Macky's leash. If we let him run loose, he might get too far ahead of us."

She jerked a nod and darted into the cabin. Her mental acuity had returned now that she was no longer in a panic, and she took the seconds necessary to stuff a pair of water bottles and packages of jerky in a small backpack. Who knew how long they would be tracking Zander and Sofie, and it was never wise to trek into the wilderness without basic essential supplies. She added extra ammunition and her small first-aid kit to the pack. Which reminded her, as much as the thought chaffed, they'd need to wait to leave until Gabe's wound was bandaged.

Fully equipped, she returned to the deck to find the SOG medic fastening a bandage around Gabe's upper arm. "You need to get that looked at in the hospital, and antibiotics administered, but that'll hold you for now." The man patted his patient's uninjured shoulder.

Gabe rose, buttoned his bloodied shirt, and pulled his equally bloodied jacket on and zipped it up. "No time now."

"You could leave the fugitive hunt to us." The team leader frowned.

Tara faced him. "You know that's not going to happen."

The man rippled his shoulders in a shrug of surrender. "The helicopter's on its way, and I can spare two deputies to accompany you."

"They'd better keep up." Gabe reached for the teddy and the leash in Tara's hand.

She gave the items to him. He attached the leash to Macky's collar, then knelt in front of the tense dog. His tail stood straight out, and the animal's every muscle quivered. Gabe put the stuffed toy under his dog's nose. The coonhound sniffed deeply in sharp yet delicate puffs.

"Go find her, boy."

Letting out a low sound like a cross between a growl and a whine, the sleek dog lunged toward the woods. Leash in hand, Gabe followed in a leap off the deck, and Tara stayed on his heels.

A heartbeat before they plunged into the trees, Tara caught the paleness of Gabe's face as he glanced behind him toward her. "Looks like he's making a beeline for the two vehicles about a mile away."

Tara clenched her jaw. "You're sure he can't use either of them."

In the dark of the woods, she could scarcely discern the outline of his large body, but she plainly heard his snort.

"Try driving off this mountain with four flat tires."

Macky carried on whuffling and snuffling ahead of them both. From the jerky way Gabe's dark shadow moved and the occasional hiss from his lips, she assumed from the jarring of his wound, the coonhound appeared to be yanking eagerly at the leash. Clearly, the scent was strong.

"Which direction do you think… Zander will go when he discovers…his transportation out of commission?"

Her words came out in huffs as their pace came nearly to a full-out run. Only the darkness and the obstruction of trees and forest debris slowed them.

"That's what we'll need Macky to tell us."

"What if he…stops running to ambush us?"

"Macky will tell us that, too. But keep your pistol ready at all times. Time to go quiet now. We'll be there soon."

Tara snapped her teeth closed against further anxious chatter and opened her ears to the forest. One thing she didn't hear was the pair of deputies the SOG leader had promised, but that didn't mean they weren't there. Either they were experts in the woods, or they were lagging behind. Either way, Gabe, Macky and she were not slowing down. Sofie was depending on them to snatch her back from a horrible fate. Tara could not, would not, let her down.

As they neared the spot where the mercs' cars were parked, Gabe spoke firmly but softly to Macky, and the dog slowed and ceased yanking the leash. He understood the dog's rush. They all loved Sofie. But if Wolf and his little captive lurked nearby, Gabe would rather approach quietly and carefully. Besides, even though he held the leash in the hand of his uninjured arm, each lunge of the coonhound had strained his injury, spearing lances of pain through his whole body.

Now, as they proceeded more slowly, the wound simply throbbed in time with his heartbeat. He ignored the discomfort, stuffed it into a mental box and put it on a shelf—there, but irrelevant—just like he'd learned to do in his days as a special operator.

Consciously probing his surroundings with his senses, Gabe caught the tension in the environment. The inhabitants of the woods were on high alert, either hiding or fleeing. No normal nocturnal sounds reached his ears—only Tara's muted breathing and Macky's soft panting. Someone a bit noisy and clumsy had been through here recently.

Half crouching, Gabe halted with a hand behind him to stop Tara, who came up on his heels. She was sharp enough on the uptake not to question him. Her warm breath feathered against the back of his neck. Winding the leash around his hand, he drew his dog close. Without looking over his shoulder, he patted his palm against Tara's jacket, indicating for her to stay put. Then, with Macky at heel position, he crept slowly forward and peered out between the trees into the clearing where the abandoned vehicles squatted, impotent, on slashed tires.

No one lingered in the area, but an infinitesimal growl from the coonhound let him know someone *had* been here recently. Or maybe they were still in the area, watching from the woods to shoot whoever showed up. *That would be us*. But Gabe wasn't about to let himself be shot—again—or anyone with him.

Kneeling, he picked up a large pine cone and tossed it underhand into the grill of the nearest vehicle. The *tink-thunk* drew no response from anyone lurking in the woods. Strong probability that Zander, knowing SOG was working with him and Tara, was doing his best to put distance between him and his kidnapped daughter and any pursuit. A guy like him would have a backup plan—someone waiting in the wings to be called in and scoop him out of here. They needed to stop the fugitive before he connected with his plan B crew.

One thing was for certain. Zander couldn't be more than a mile ahead of them in any direction. Time to find out which one.

Gabe rubbed between Macky's ears and looked into the hound's luminous brown eyes. "Find her, boy. Let's get Sofie."

He rose and released the leash's coils but did not let the tether go. Rather he allowed Macky to pull him into the clearing. Offering no direction, he followed the dog as he sniffed the ground, then stuck his nose in the air and inhaled. The cycle repeated until they came around the farthest side of the parking area.

Then, a deep bay surged from Macky's throat, and he was off. Back to the jerking and lunging. Gabe's heart surged into his throat as he followed his dog and the coonhound's unerring nose. Tara's footfalls padded hard on his heels.

He glanced back at her anxious face reflecting in the moon's glow. "We're close." He panted. "Macky doesn't bay unless the quarry is well within reach."

"Don't slow down…for me. Sofie is all that matters."

Gabe turned his entire concentration on following his dog safely and swiftly, but apprehension gnawed at the back of his mind. Macky's throaty bay would have let their quarry know a hound was on his trail, and not far behind. What might a desperate narcissist do to an innocent in his power when faced with capture and failure to achieve his goal?

Tara's foot caught on an unseen root sticking up from the forest floor, and she tumbled forward with a muted cry. She landed hard on the spongy ground. Dried pine needles pricked her face and hands, as the air whooshed from her lungs. Scrambling to her feet, she gave herself a shake of self-disgust. *Way to go, graceful.* She had no time for face-plants. Gabe and Macky were drawing ahead of her.

Were they closing in on their quarry? Other than the evidence delivered by Macky's nose, she'd seen no sign of Zander and Sofie's passing this way.

And then she did.

A tuft of fabric from Sofie's blanket hung from a sharp needleless pine branch attached to a dead tree that leaned halfway across the game trail they seemed to be following.

Tara plucked the sign of hope from the branch and clutched it in her fist as she plunged onward. Gabe and Macky were so far ahead now that she couldn't see them but only hear sporadic hints of their swift passage. The man and his dog knew how to negotiate the woods in near silence.

How much lead did the kidnapper have on them? Every nerve in Tara's body stood on end. *Please, God.*

Then a familiar cry reaches her ears. Faint. Distant. But distinct.

*Sofie, we're coming for you, baby.*

Fresh strength surged through Tara's limbs, and her senses leaped to high alert. She rammed like a moose between tangled bushes, jumped like a mustang around clumps of deadfall and then soared like a mule deer across jutting rocks. The ground passed beneath her feet in a blur. If she were being scratched or cut by burs or branches, she remained unaware and uncaring. Any obstacle nature threw in her way, she'd plow through, around or over like a mama grizzly on a mission.

Ahead, Macky erupted in frenzied baying. The sound sang in Tara's veins, urging her onward. What a frightening noise to the dog's quarry, but an encouragement to her.

All at once, she burst from the tree line and skidded to an abrupt halt, the breath sawing in her lungs. The moon, dipping low, stood directly behind a dark figure, standing only a few feet from a cliff's edge. The man gripped a wriggling, fussing Sofie—wrapped like a burrito in her blanket—under one arm, like she was nothing but an inanimate package. He pointed a gun at Gabe, though his head swiveled back and forth between the man and a slavering, pacing Macky.

"Not a step closer." The black outline waggled its weapon.

Tara froze in place. She'd never heard the suave Zander's voice carry such a rough edge. Desperate people did unthinkable things. Gabe and she needed to deescalate the situation. But how?

"Glad you could join us, *Auntie*." Fury and contempt dripped from the man's tone. "You know me. You know I'll do it."

"Do what?" Dread pinched Tara's heart.

"Call that dog off, all of you back away, and let me go with my daughter, or I'll fling her over the edge."

Tara's mouth went bone-dry, and bile burned her throat. Zander Wolf lived by the code that if he was to be denied something, then he'd make sure no one else could have it, either. That included destroying his ex-wife. the mother of his child, and now he intended to do the same to the little girl herself.

Gripping his gun in his right hand, Gabe kept the weapon trained on Wolf. He didn't trust the guy not to take a shot at one of them. He needed to create a distraction. What that might be, he was unsure. Yet. Too many moving parts in this situation. Unpredictable factors that could abruptly tip the scales toward life or death.

"Okay, you win."

From his adversary's grunt, he assumed those words squared with the guy's need to dominate. So far, so good. Gabe patted the air with his free hand and spoke softly to Macky.

As they'd neared their quarry, Gabe had let the dog off the leash, and the coonhound had cornered the prey, just like he was trained to do. Now, at Gabe's word, the animal stopped pacing and stood statue-still a half dozen feet away from his master's side. The dog's head remained high, snout and steely stare fixed on the man who held Sofie.

"He won't do anything unless I tell him." Gabe took a half step backward, though Tara apparently moved forward, because she appeared at his side.

Her whole body quivered as if an electrical current flowed through her. *Don't do anything desperate, sweetheart.* Somewhere in the back of his mind, the endearment slipping through his thoughts registered, but he didn't have the time to dwell on the affection it implied.

Tara took another step forward, and Gabe restrained himself from trying to grab her. The sudden movement could result in catastrophe.

"Uh-uh-uh!" Wolf trained the gun toward Tara while turning his body slightly into a position that suggested a simple fling of his arm would toss Sofie over the edge into the gorge that lay who knew how far below.

"How did you find us again?" Tara's words were strained, but the tone indicated control.

Gabe swallowed an inner cheer. There was the trained US deputy marshal. Keep the fugitive talking. Engage. Create distractions, which meant opportunities.

Wolf barked a laugh. "Did you think there was only *one* tracker in that bear?"

At the barest flick of Gabe's wrist, Macky slunk like mist closer to their target.

"I'm leaving now." Zander took a side step. "And you're going to let me."

A choked sound came from Tara. "Please, I just want to kiss her goodbye."

"Forget it." Wolf called Tara an insulting name. "You've caused me enough problems. I'm going to end—"

A sleek rocket of fur and fangs went airborne and leaped obliquely in front of the ruthless criminal mastermind, snagging Sofie's blanket and pajamas in his jaws and yanking her out of the man's grasp. Twisting, Macky hit the ground on his back with the toddler between his legs and then rolled with her top over tail.

Wolf yelped, Sofie wailed, Tara screamed and Gabe pulled the trigger simultaneously with their adversary. A bullet hissed past Gabe's head, all but burning his ear.

Wolf staggered backward one step too far. Abruptly, the man toppled. A blank abyss swallowed him. His short-lived howl did his namesake proud—part rage, part disbelief and part horror. Then silence fell.

No one remaining on the cliff's edge moved. Almost not daring to breathe, Gabe's gaze found his dog comforting a softly weeping Sofie, then located Tara, rigid and open-mouthed, staring at the spot where her nemesis had stood so defiantly a second ago. She released a deep groan, and a visible tremor ran through her. A moment later, she dashed for her niece, flung herself down and wrapped the child in her arms, unashamedly bawling.

Gabe went to them, tossed his gun aside, fell to his knees and gathered them both in his arms. Hot wetness blazed trails down his cheeks as Macky danced around them, licking first one face and then another and another. In the next moment, Tara let out a watery giggle, and Sofie started babbling about the "doggy," tears and fears apparently forgotten.

If Gabe's heart got any lighter, it would become a helium balloon, and they would all float away wrapped around each other. He planned to revel in this moment of liberation. Tomorrow, he could worry about what the end of their flight and fight for freedom meant for the future. Did he dare hope the goodbyes would not be final?

# SIXTEEN

Stomach awash with butterflies, Tara walked slowly across the pavement toward a particular storage unit in a row of them. With one hand, she guided a small wheeled suitcase with a diaper bag attached to the handle, and with the other, she held her niece's little hand. The child toddled along beside her, relaxed in the pleasantly cool, sunny weather. Winter's premature attempt to foreshorten fall seemed to have been foiled for now, and puff jackets and jeans were enough to keep them warm.

A beat-up truck that used to be white but was now black stood on the tarmac outside the target unit's raised garage-style door. A metallic clatter came from inside the unit, and then a familiar tall, sturdy figure stepped outside with a sleek four-legged creature at his side.

Macky let out a welcoming *woof*, trotted straight to the little girl and began licking her cheeks. Giggling, Sofie threw her arms around the dog's neck.

"'Acky, 'acky'" she squealed.

Tara couldn't hold back a smile. Sofie had been saying more words in the past twenty-four hours than she had since Tara took custody of her. Yesterday, at nap time, she'd even asked insistently for 'Acky and 'Abe. The startling phenomenon led Tara to stop torturing herself with the question of whether Gabe might prefer the people who caused him so much upheaval and danger to be gone from his life, and instead to seek him out today. The child's shell of confusion and grief seemed to have cracked, just like Tara's, and now, if she read her niece right, they both seemed to be looking more to the future rather than dwelling in the past. Of course, depending on the results of her interaction with Gabe this morning, a setback could happen.

A full day and a night had passed since the events on the mountain that ended in Zander Wolf's demise. Law enforcement interviews, report-writing, meetings, resting and bonding with her niece had occupied that time. So many details had to be handled. At least, the owner of the bullet-riddled Airbnb was going to get his investment back. The US Marshals Service planned to purchase the property and renovate it into a safe house.

In all the hubbub, she and Gabe had hardly found an opportunity to speak together. Now, before she took Sofie home, she needed to hear Gabe's thoughts on what came next. Amicable parting or…what?

Tara stared at him and swallowed against a tight throat. "Hi, there."

Did the greeting come out nonchalant or just strangled?

"Hi, yourself."

Okay, probably strangled, because his sounded the same.

She took a gulp of the crisp air. "Getting ready to haul your car home?"

"Not exactly." He shook his head. "How about you? Do you have a ride?" His expression became stricken. "I mean, I was going to call you about my plans, you know. Not just disappear, but it never occurred to me that—"

"No, you don't owe us transportation, but I did want to see you again."

Was Tara mistaken, or did something like hope flicker across his face?

He pulled his shoulders back. "If you don't mind waiting, I'd be happy to pick you up here in a couple of days, and we could ride back to Montana together. Great Falls isn't that far out of my way."

Understanding clicked inside Tara, and she smiled. "You're going to the car show."

Shifting from foot to foot, he glanced over his shoulder toward the storage unit that held the car and trailer. "At this point, I'll only make it for the final day, but yeah, I really want to show up and greet Dad's friends, let them know what happened. He loved those people, and they loved him back. I think maybe they'll be able to—"

"Give you a fuller picture of your father than the parent-child relationship made possible."

Gabe's smile broke out and warmed Tara to her toes. "You put that exactly right. Part of the coming-to-terms-with-loss process. And I want to tell *you* thanks, also."

"For what?"

"Listening to my story about losing my team. Understanding. Not judging. I'd bottled up the hurt and tried to pretend it wasn't there. All that did was turn me into a lonely curmudgeon."

Tara laughed. "Can you *be* a curmudgeon in your early thirties?"

"Not sure there's an age limit in the definition." He offered a crooked grin and scratched his head.

"So-o-o." Tara echoed his foot-shifting behavior. "Now that Sofie and I are out of danger, would you prefer this trek to be a solo endeavor?"

The question seemed to stun Gabe, and he stared at her blankly.

Then his face lit up. "You *want* to come with me?"

Tara lowered her gaze and motioned toward Sofie and Macky, who were still making nice with each other. "Far be it from me to part a dog from his pet toddler."

Gabe adopted a mock frown and tapped his pursed lips with a finger. "Come to think of it, he has been acting like he's got toddler withdrawal symptoms. Let's load up. Looks like you're ready to go, and the car seat is still in the back of my truck."

Within an hour, they were on the road, singing along with Oldies like they'd never been rudely interrupted by people with bad intentions.

"I like this," Gabe announced as they crossed into Utah.

"Me, too." Tara nodded. Then she looked over her shoulder to find Macky sleeping with his head on a slumbering toddler's lap. "I think they're happy also."

Silence fell, mostly contented, but Gabe shifted in his seat like he had something on his mind.

"Go ahead and ask." Tara fixed him with a steady gaze.

He took a long breath and let it out. "I don't mean to be nosy, but what will you do when you get home? Go back to deputy work?"

"Good question, and not nosy. You care about Sofie, too. But no." Tara shook her head. "My niece has been through too much upheaval in her life for me to continue in a career with unstable hours and a high degree of danger. I'm still praying about it, but I'm leaning toward hanging up my badge, maybe going back to school online. Then I can be home with her, at least until she's ready to ease into school years herself. I'm not hurting for money—Sofie, either. I've still got most of my parents' life insurance legacy, and my sister had a policy that left her daughter fixed for a good education down the line."

"Sounds like you've been doing a lot of thinking over the past day or two."

Tara shook her head. "These thoughts have been percolating for a while, but I couldn't act on them until the mess with you-know-who was resolved. For the outcome of *that* seemingly impossible situation, you have my undying gratitude for your courage and sacrifice. Without you, I don't know if we—" She gulped and held back a rush of tears.

Gabe's warm hand closed around hers, and she responded by hanging on tight.

"I have to confess." She swallowed again. "I used to think I didn't want to depend on anyone, not even God. But here I am today, praying about every little thing. And with you… I don't want to go back to being just me and Sofie anymore."

"Do you mean it?" The grip on her hand became almost painful. "You'd let this ex-curmudgeon into your lives? Like permanently?"

"What do you think of this plan?" She swiveled toward him. "How about you keep the driveway clear this winter at my cabin up near where you live. Sofie and I will take up residence there. We'll be close and—"

"Macky and I will court Sofie and you until—"

"We become a family. I have to confess I'm already in love with you, so the courting doesn't need to take long."

Under Gabe's steady guidance, the vehicle slowed, and they pulled off into a wayside rest. Tara stayed silent, anticipation simmering under the surface, as he parked the rig in a remote corner of the lot.

She stared into his hazel eyes, tinted more brownish gold than green, in this solemn moment.

"What do you think of my proposal?" Her question emerged as a husky murmur.

"I love you, too, and I accept." His whispered answer brimmed with longing and promise.

Gabe's strong arms pulled Tara close. She lifted her head to receive his warm kiss—the first of what she knew with all her heart would be many in the years to come.

* * * * *

Dear Reader,

There is no greater detriment to a child than a parent who passes on a legacy of wickedness. Conversely, a parent (or parent substitute) who loves their children and trains them in godly character is priceless.

At first, Tara's personal crisis of faith leaves her relying on her own resources as a parent and protector, but gradually she learns to lean on God for strength and ability. Painful loss has isolated Gabe from relationships. Tara and Sofie draw him back into human connection. Though neither is Sofie's biological parent, they fill the roles God intended, proving that true parents are those who do the work with loving hearts.

I enjoy hearing from my readers. My email address is jnelson@jillelizabethnelson.com. I can also be contacted through my Facebook page: Facebook.com/JillElizabeth-Nelson.Author.

Abundant Blessings,
*Jill*